R.

She must be

His hands fell away from her as if her arms were on fire.

His first thought was that Uncle Edward had been miraculously—undeservedly—blessed. She was beautiful, her fragile beauty shining through her exhaustion. The deep circles under her eyes only highlighted the blue that he knew would be bright when unclouded by fatigue.

"Excuse me." A voice behind her spoke, and a woman, her ebony hair edged with silver, leaned over the young lady's shoulder. Her eyes were worried. "I'm looking for Edward Collier. I understood he would be here." The last words were more a question than a statement.

The pieces of the world fell into place, and he was absurdly glad to have the knowledge that the damsel with the enchanting blue eyes was not his uncle's mail-order bride.

His relief had nothing to do with the rosy cheeks and the bright pink lips. Professor Barkley discouraged romantic entanglements, so love was definitely not going to have a place in Silas Collier's heart. No, not at all.

In first grade, **JANET SPAETH** was asked to write a summary of a story about a family making maple syrup. She wrote all during class, through morning recess, lunch, and afternoon recess, and asked to stay after school. When the teacher pointed out that a summary was supposed to be shorter than the original story, Janet explained that she didn't feel the readers knew the characters well enough, so she was expanding on what was in the first-grade reader. Thus a writer was born. She lives in the Midwest and loves to travel, but to her, the happiest word in the English language is *home*.

Books by Janet Spaeth

HEARTSONG PRESENTS
HP458—Candy Cane Calaboose
HP522—Angel's Roost
HP679—Rose Kelly

Remembrance

Janet Spaeth

Heartsong Presents

To Kevin, always. . .and forever

A note from the Author:
I love to hear from my readers! You may correspond with me by writing:

Janet Spaeth
Author Relations
PO Box 721
Uhrichsville, OH 44683

ISBN 978-1-60260-356-1

REMEMBRANCE

All scripture quotations are taken from the King James Version of the Bible.

All of the characters and events in this book are fictitious. Any resemblance to actual persons, living or dead, or to actual events is purely coincidental.

Our mission is to publish and distribute inspirational products offering exceptional value and biblical encouragement to the masses.

PRINTED IN THE U.S.A.

one

On the way to Remembrance, Minnesota,
January 1886

Eliza Davis drew her coat a little closer around her. The early winter night closed in on the darkened railroad car like a thick woolen wrap. The *chicketta-ticketta* of the wheels clicked out a regular beat, but she couldn't sleep. Snow flurries, lit by starlight, fluffed beside the windows as the train sped onward.

Home. She was going home. There was a good feeling about this, something that almost kindled the dead corner of her heart where love had once lived.

No one knew she was coming. She'd done the only thing she could think of in the thin dawn hours in the cold room where she'd lived in St. Paul. She hadn't packed, other than snatching the worn Bible from the table, seizing a few last-minute items from her bureau, and throwing some clothing into the big carpetbag that belonged to her father.

Haste had been of utmost importance—at least at the time it had seemed so. Now that miles separated her from Blaine Loring, she was already feeling calmer.

He became everything to her, and everything became his. It was a dangerous combination.

How had her life spiraled so badly out of control?

At first, her plan to establish herself as a fine seamstress in St. Paul had gone well. She quickly found employment as an assistant to one of the most respected tailoring establishments in the growing city. Her skills quickly took her far. She opened her own business within a short time, sewing fancy dresses for the women of wealth who appreciated her attention to the tiniest details.

Soon she met some of the most well-known people in Minnesota's capital, and the stars in her eyes grew bigger and brighter, blinding her to the reality of her world.

Blaine Loring slithered into her life, saw her glittering ambition, and stole her heart. He had money to spend, and spend he did. Whenever he came into the tailor shop, he'd slip a gift to her, once a fine silk scarf as soft and delicate as a windswept whisper, once a tiny gold locket on a thin linked chain.

He had promises, one after the other, and with their power, she let herself be swept along like a leaf on a wild torrent. She wouldn't stay a seamstress, he told her again and again. She was too good for that. Her place was on Summit Avenue, the splendid street in St. Paul lined with the largest, stateliest houses she'd ever seen.

For a while, she let herself believe that she might actually one day be a fine lady on Summit Avenue. One foot inside the mansions lining the street set that desire firmly upon her heart. She'd never seen such sumptuous homes, such tasteful wealth.

Earlier this evening it had all come to an end.

Eliza shifted uncomfortably on the cracked leather seat of the train. It was a horrible memory.

She simply went to return a paper she found on the floor of the shop after he left, a list of investors she knew he needed for a meeting that night, and found him shadowed in the back door of the club he frequented, his arms wrapped around a young woman as he murmured familiar words to her.

That had been bad enough, but then—

She paused in her mental recitation of the night, not wanting to go further but unable to stop, and the images continued.

She must have gasped, because he turned to her, and in the faint reflection of the moon, his eyes hardened to coal.

"You!" he snarled, and then he laughed, a humorless sound that made the young woman in his embrace giggle. "You have more alley cat in you than I'd guessed, following me the way you do. Shoo! Scat!"

His words threw ice shards into her soul, and she ran back to her room, tossed some of her belongings into a bag, and went to the train station.

"Where to?" the agent asked, and the answer rose quickly to her lips.

"Remembrance." She hadn't been there for years, but it was the only other place she knew as her home, besides St. Paul. Her memories of it were warm and comforting.

Yes, she was headed in the right direction, back to Remembrance, back to the home in the north woods of Minnesota where the world was small and safe and God-fearing.

The train swayed as a gust of wind struck them. Eliza glanced outside. The snowflakes were coming faster, and no longer falling straight down.

She shut her eyes for a quick prayer. *Please, God, calm the winds. I can't be delayed in getting home.*

She was going home, laden not with success but with secrets, secrets that could change the way they viewed her.

Remembrance was on the edge of the prairie, where the land suddenly turned to forest. She loved that about the little town, how it had the best of both possible worlds. The prairie land stretched to the west, all the way to the horizon, and the forests sprang up to the east, each tree reaching for heaven.

When she left fifteen years ago, summer had just touched

the prairie with newborn green. Baby rabbits bounced across the open lands, growing, well fed on the fresh grasses and budding flowers.

But it hadn't held any happiness for her father, not after her mother got sick, and he traded in the clean country town for a city clogged with soot and grime. Oh, not all of it, she had to admit. Parts of St. Paul were lovely—amazingly so, in fact.

❧

"Excuse me." The older woman across the aisle from her spoke softly so as not to wake the others. "Would you like a muffin? I have extra, and the trip is long yet."

Eliza shook her head. "No, thank you. I don't seem to have an appetite at the moment."

The woman nodded sympathetically. "Traveling does that."

Eliza sized her up quickly. She looked safe. One thing she'd discovered quickly about Blaine was that his friends usually looked as sleazy as they were. Why hadn't she seen that earlier?

But she reminded herself that this was probably all part of God's plan. She couldn't see it now, but at some point, everything would make sense. That was one promise she could believe.

Her stomach growled loudly, reminding her that she hadn't eaten in several hours.

The woman smiled encouragingly and offered the pastry again. "Please, help yourself."

"Thank you very much," Eliza said, accepting the muffin. It smelled wonderful.

"Are you going far?"

"I'm going to Remembrance. I do appreciate the muffin. I don't know when I'd be able to eat, now that I think about it. I hadn't planned that far ahead."

The woman nodded but didn't inquire.

"Remembrance is small, too small to have a restaurant like I'd find in St. Paul. There are seven buildings downtown," Eliza said, nearly reciting it as a litany. "One is white-painted wood, and one is new-lumber brown, and one is grayed from the wind. Two are red brick. The other two are brown and gray speckled brick. There is a church, and a school, and a general store. A doctor's office, a bank, and a station. The last one is still empty."

"Not anymore." Her traveling companion spoke.

"You know Remembrance?" Eliza sat up. There was something in the Bible about news from home, how good it felt. It seemed as if her heart were being washed.

"I'm on my way to Remembrance myself. I'm Hyacinth Mason."

Eliza relaxed at the friendliness of the woman's voice. "It's good to meet you, Mrs. Mason."

"Please, call me Hyacinth. I'm expecting we'll be friends in Remembrance."

The warmth of her voice reminded Eliza how much more Blaine had stolen from her—her friends. She hadn't had a true friend since she'd met Blaine. With him, everything and everyone was business. All of her friendships, under his guidance, were mined as investment possibilities.

"I hope so. It's been a while since I've been to Remembrance," Eliza said. "Do you live there now?"

The woman smiled, and suddenly she looked years younger than her true age, which Eliza estimated to be around fifty-five or sixty. "I'm on my way to meet someone. I'm hoping that he and I might find a life together."

"Excuse me?" The woman's words made no sense to Eliza.

Hyacinth smiled. "We haven't met face-to-face. I'm from Chicago. We've corresponded for some time, though, and he convinced me to come join him in Remembrance. If all goes well, we plan to get married."

"You came from Illinois to marry someone you haven't met?" Eliza couldn't stop the question. It seemed too outrageous. Marrying someone, anyone, was massively important, even if you'd known the person all your life. She knew that well enough herself. But marrying someone you'd never met. . . !

"I knew his heart, and that was the most important thing." Hyacinth looked at Eliza and laughed. "I can see by your face that you are unconvinced. Haven't you ever been in love?"

Eliza's face burned. This was a question she would not, or maybe could not, answer. Instead, she focused on breaking off a bit of the muffin and chewing it slowly. "I have loved," she stated simply.

Suddenly exhaustion washed over her, and she rested her head against the railroad car's seat. Hyacinth smiled gently at her and patted her hand. "I can see you're tired, my dear. Remembrance isn't far away, perhaps two hours more. Go ahead and rest. Get some sleep."

It should have been no surprise, the way God put Hyacinth Mason in the same car with her. She was the perfect traveling companion, calm and caring and watchful.

Blaine Loring stole Eliza's few last moments of wakefulness. He quickly swept into her life like the winter wind, and equally quickly swept away her heart. . .and her good sense. His elegant clothing and regal demeanor bore an aura of glamour, and like a moth to the flame, she was drawn to the small light they offered.

A way out of a life of dressmaking. An exit from the mundane. Excitement.

That was what she had wished for. That was, unfortunately, exactly what she had gotten.

✍

Silas paced edgily. The thin boards of the station didn't do much to protect him from the cold or the hungry wind that sought and found each crack in the walls.

This was a bad idea. In a world filled with good ideas, why did his uncle have to choose this? People didn't fall in love with words on the page. That was ridiculous. Usually his uncle was a sane, normal man. Love did something terrible to him.

Now Uncle Edward was at home, his foot swathed in a bandage. He'd been adding some furbelow over the frame of the front door—a carved piece of plaster flowers, most odd— when he lost his balance and tumbled to the floor, snapping his ankle when he hit the floor.

And Silas blamed it all on love. It made idiots of perfectly normal people. Now someone like himself, who was under- taking a serious program of study, *Professor Barkley's Patented Five Year Plan for Success*, would never make such a mistake. He sighed and thanked the Lord for leading him to the small booklet, which he found stuck in the desk drawer in his room at his uncle's house.

Hyacinth. What kind of name was that? She was un- doubtedly some fortune hunter, a woman of insubstantial means, out to make her way on the coattails of his uncle's hard work.

The wind increased its howl, and Silas instinctively shrugged deeper into his buffalo robe. At least Uncle Edward had the sense to live in town. He wouldn't want to face the prairie on a night like this, when the sky and the earth blended into one whirling stretch of white.

He'd asked his uncle to describe his mail-order bride, but all he'd gotten in response was a rather coy reminder that

Hyacinth wasn't his bride yet. This was, as Uncle Edward pointed out, simply an extended visit, with perhaps an eye on potential matrimony.

Silas was not fooled. Potential matrimony, indeed. His uncle planned to marry Hyacinth. Perhaps the only question was whether Hyacinth planned to marry his uncle.

It was enough to curdle his blood. Love. Who needed it?

Over the whine of the wind, the train shrilled the announcement that it was headed into town.

Usually it was a lonesome sound as the train whistle cut across the prairie, but tonight its sound filled the snow-locked town with life. Tonight the train would stop in Remembrance.

He stopped his striding back and forth. If he kept this up, he'd wear a hole in the floorboards.

The train chugged its way to a stop, and he got ready to brave the cold. . .and Hyacinth.

He raised the collar of his coat and tucked his chin down deep inside the rich brown fur. He'd smelled better things than this buffalo robe, but nothing could beat it for warmth.

He opened the door of the station to go out and carry in Hyacinth's bags. A woman like her would probably expect that. She was undoubtedly too fragile to see to her own baggage.

A gust of wind blew in, and a young woman staggered in on its force, right into the front of his buffalo robe. Instinctively he reached out to steady her, and for just a minute he allowed himself to revel in the sensation of holding a woman in his arms—even if they were separated by a good two inches of wild fur and thick woolen fabric.

She smelled better than his coat, too. It took him a moment to realize that she smelled like blueberries and. . .what was that indefinable smell? Ah, soap.

How on earth did she manage to smell like blueberries?

She looked up at him, and he knew the answer. A crumb was somehow attached to her cheek—how it managed to stay in the wind was a mystery. It had been a long time since he'd eaten a blueberry muffin.

He tried not to think about that, or about the scent of soap, or the way she felt in his arms.

She must be Hyacinth.

His hands fell away from her as if her arms were on fire.

His first thought was that Uncle Edward had been miraculously—undeservedly—blessed. She was beautiful, her fragile beauty shining through her exhaustion. The deep circles under her eyes only highlighted the blue that he knew would be bright when unclouded by fatigue.

"Excuse me." A voice behind her spoke, and a woman, her ebony hair edged with silver, leaned over the young lady's shoulder. Her eyes were worried. "I'm looking for Edward Collier. I understood he would be here." The last words were more a question than a statement.

The pieces of the world fell into place, and he was absurdly glad to have the knowledge that the damsel with the enchanting blue eyes was not his uncle's mail-order bride.

His relief had nothing to do with the rosy cheeks and the bright pink lips. Professor Barkley discouraged romantic entanglements, so love was definitely not going to have a place in Silas Collier's heart. No, not at all.

two

Eliza smoothed the front of her coat, her nervous fingers wiping away the imprint of this man's embrace. The last time—the only time—she'd been that close to a man's chest, she had been struggling for her honor. The memory brought a quick, sour taste to her mouth.

But she felt she could trust this fellow. His cinnamon-colored hair was neatly trimmed, and his buffalo robe must have been chosen for function rather than style. His face, reddened with embarrassment, indicated that he was not the same kind of beast that Blaine Loring was—*he* would have taken full advantage of having a woman clasped that tightly to him.

This man's forehead was furrowed with confusion. He took off his wire-rimmed glasses, wiped them, and stuck them back on his nose. Then he cleared his throat. "Excuse me. My name is Silas Collier, and I am to meet a Mrs. Hyacinth Mason. Might either of you be Mrs. Mason?"

Hyacinth stepped forward. "I'm Hyacinth Mason. Edward Collier—"

A man, his hair the same dark gold as Silas's but lightened with gray, laboriously hobbled toward them, his face glowing with obvious anticipation. He looked vaguely familiar; Eliza must have known him when she was a child. "Hyacinth? Hyacinth? Is it truly you?" His leg and ankle were wrapped, and he balanced himself—badly—with a wooden crutch.

"Uncle Edward, didn't I tell you to stay home?" Silas reached to help him but was waved away impatiently.

"How could I stay away from seeing my Hyacinth? Hyacinth, oh, Hyacinth, how long I have waited for this moment!" The older man's eyes glowed.

Eliza couldn't keep her eyes off the unfolding scene. It was like something out of a book, a story of love lost and found and told with great drama.

Hyacinth ran toward the man. "Edward? Oh, Edward, what has happened to your precious limb?"

Silas coughed. " 'Precious limb'?"

Eliza couldn't help herself. She knew she shouldn't find this so funny, but she was so tired that she had no self-control left. *Precious limb, indeed.* She choked back her laughter and tried to hide it in a series of coughs that probably fooled no one.

"Crazy woman," Silas muttered.

She leaned over and said, in a stage whisper, "Hyacinth seems very smitten."

Silas shook his head, as the older couple cooed over each other like love-struck teenagers. "I can't think this is a good thing."

"What, that his precious limb is broken?"

"That, and the fact that he's so overtaken with the idea of having found his true helpmate in Hyacinth that he's been remodeling the house, which was just fine to begin with, and two days ago he took a dive off a ladder while installing a decorative doodad on the door and managed to crack his 'precious limb.'"

"The limb will heal," she said gently.

"Do hearts?" he responded cryptically.

She didn't have an answer for that.

The couple on the other side of the station stood up, their arms linked together, and slowly made their way toward Silas and Eliza.

"Mrs. Mason, we've arranged to have you stay at Mrs. Adams's Boardinghouse. I'm sorry, I didn't know your daughter was coming, too."

"Oh, bless your heart, as honored as I'd be to have her as my own, she and I just met on the train." Hyacinth reached over and squeezed Eliza's arm as Silas reached for her bag. "I'm hoping that she and I will become good friends, and that she'll become a part of the Collier family, too."

Eliza froze, and even without moving her eyes, she saw Silas's reaction. He, too, stopped mid-motion, his arm halfway to her bag, his mouth agape.

Hyacinth broke the ice of the moment by laughing. "Well, that's not exactly what I meant. Of course we don't want her to be part of the family." She stopped as Silas stood up, his face flooded with crimson. "That's not right. I mean she could be, and—Oh, someone give me a shovel. I'm digging this hole way too fast!"

Eliza swallowed. This wasn't going at all the way she'd featured it would. In her hurried plans, she'd imagined that she'd come to Remembrance and hide while she gathered her dreams about her. She hadn't even thought where she might stay.

"Actually, I'll be on my way now—" she began, but Silas interrupted her.

"Please, allow me. The boardinghouse is just across the road and down a bit, and I'm taking Mrs. Mason there anyway, so one more in the wagon is no trouble." He picked up Hyacinth's bag in one hand and hers in the other, and once again, his warm golden eyes met hers. "So, Miss—" He stopped. "I'm sorry, I don't know your name."

"Davis. Eliza Davis. And I'm pleased to meet you."

Color washed over his face. "Thank you. I'm glad to meet

you, too." He cleared his throat. "Shall we go?"

They left the little station and went outside. Snowflakes sparkled through the air, turning to water as soon as they touched her skin. Silas helped her into the wagon and handed her a lap robe to cover her legs and feet. She tucked herself under as much as she could, burying her hands in the blanket's warmth. She sat, trying to ignore the couple behind her as they spoke soft words that lilted in the night air.

Beside her, Silas stared straight ahead as he led the horse away from the station and down the snow-covered road.

The incongruity of her situation was almost overwhelming. Within twenty-four hours, or just a bit over it, she'd watched her romance destroyed, abandoned her home and business, left the city she'd called home for fifteen years, returned to a place she obviously hadn't remembered at all well, and now she was sitting in a wagon with people she didn't know, being led to a place she'd never seen.

She'd had no plans at all when she'd left the city in a heartbroken rush, and headed for what seemed to be home—to Remembrance.

Under the cover of darkness, she peeked at Silas. He could be a murderer for all she knew, and she'd willingly gotten in the wagon with him and let him take her to a place she knew nothing about, where she would stay. She had clearly gone off her bearings to trust him so completely, but there was just something about him, something about those cider-colored eyes behind the staid wire-rimmed glasses, that made her feel comfortable with her decision to go with him.

She was in Remembrance. She hugged the thought to her. Remembrance!

Her eyes couldn't take in enough of the small town. It had changed so much since she'd left, and what she hadn't been old enough to recall, her mind created. The school had seemed big, but now it looked small. The white house on the corner with the blue shutters—hadn't that been a small reddish house before? And she didn't remember the mercantile being on that street at all.

The moon was almost full, illuminating the town as they drove to the boardinghouse.

It wasn't far. Soon Silas brought the wagon to a stop and leaped out.

"My uncle and I would be pleased to have both of you come to supper tomorrow evening," he said as he lifted the bags from the wagon. "By the way, if you've a mind to attend services in the morning, the church is not at all far from Mrs. Adams's place. She usually brings over the churchgoers."

Edward snorted. "*Usually?* Humph. Like they have a choice."

Eliza sat in the wagon, reluctant to leave the comfortable cocoon of the lap robe, and studied the building where she'd begin her new life in Remembrance.

The boardinghouse was large, its white paint reflecting the moon's glow with a dazzling brilliance. Blue shutters framed wide windows that were draped with patterned curtains. One curtain fluttered a bit. Someone inside had taken notice of their arrival.

"I don't intend to carry you in." Silas's voice broke her reverie, and she laughed.

"I suppose!" She took Silas's hand almost absently as she got out of the wagon and, while Hyacinth and Edward murmured reluctant good-nights, she walked up the steps to the front door, with Silas behind her, bearing the bags.

Mrs. Adams met them there, a single lantern illuminating the entry to the boardinghouse. Her steel gray hair bristled out at odd angles, and her barely stifled yawn indicated that they'd woken her up.

"I'll take them from here," Mrs. Adams said, reaching for the bags and taking one in each hand. "You know my rules, Silas Collier. There'll be no men in this house this time of night. Good evening."

He barely had a chance to lift his hand in farewell before the door slammed on him. "Too late for gentlemen to be here," Mrs. Adams grumbled. "I run a decent house here, and there'll be none of that, thank you very much. By the way, I don't rent rooms to just anyone."

The landlady sighed and walked over to a tall desk near the front door. She unlocked the desk and removed a ledger book. "I'm going to need some information about you both. Who you are, and how long you plan to stay. Lodging is fifty cents a week, in advance. Hyacinth Mason, I have your particulars, but not yours." She stared at Eliza. "Who are you?"

"I'm Eliza Davis, and I will need a room until I find a place to live." Eliza had no idea what else she should say.

Mrs. Adams nodded, her gaze still locked onto Eliza's face. Perspiration began to break out under Eliza's coat. It was horribly uncomfortable, being overtly examined like this.

"You're going to stay in Remembrance?" Mrs. Adams said at last.

"I hope to."

"I see. Well, fill this out." She pushed the ledger toward Eliza and watched as Eliza filled in her name and address.

"St. Paul, I see," Mrs. Adams said, looking at the entry.

"I've left there. That was my last address."

For a moment, the landlady didn't speak, and then she said, "Payment in advance," and held out her hand.

Eliza opened her coin purse and withdrew fifty cents. Mrs.

Adams took it, along with Hyacinth's money, and the coins vanished into a tin in the desk. The woman closed the desk and locked it.

"Now, I'll take you to your rooms. You two are my only boarders at the moment, so there's no hiding in the crowd. Your rooms are on the second floor, Mrs. Mason, you're first on the left, and Miss Davis, you're next to her. Here are the rules. Breakfast is served at seven. On the dot. You're late, you've missed it. Dinner is at noon. Supper at six. I don't tolerate stragglers."

As the three of them climbed the stairs, Mrs. Adams continued. "These doors lock at nine each night. You're not in by then, you're out. I'll have your bags packed and on the front steps by sunrise the next morning."

A pin had worked its way free from the stiff gray hair coiled at the nape of the landlady's neck, and Eliza watched it in fascination as it swung back and forth, keeping time with Mrs. Adams's verbal list.

"Church every Sunday. Bell rings at eight, service begins half an hour later. You're expected to be there," she continued with her list as they neared the top of the stairs. The hairpin had nearly worked its way free. "No men guests, except in the parlor, and then just on Saturday and Sunday afternoons between three and five. Dress and act modestly, and that means no taking the Lord's name in vain. Those are the rules."

The silver hairpin dangled dangerously, and just as it was about to tumble down the collar of Mrs. Adams's blue calico wrapper, the woman dropped the bags at the first door and reached up to resecure the wayward pin. "And no animals, not a cat, not a dog, not a chicken."

Eliza looked at Hyacinth, which was a mistake. Hyacinth rolled her eyes, and a stream of laughter began to bubble up.

She disguised it with a quick cough, which apparently didn't fool Mrs. Adams, who harrumphed.

"You don't have to stay here. But I'll warn you, I'm the only boardinghouse in town."

"Yes, ma'am," Eliza said meekly. She didn't trust herself to say more.

"You have my word, Mrs. Adams," Hyacinth said.

Mrs. Adams turned and faced Hyacinth. "You're that mail-order woman."

"I have been corresponding with Mr. Edward Collier." The color rose in Hyacinth's face.

"Humph." Mrs. Adams considered her guest silently before turning to open the door. "I don't hold with that kind of nonsense, but you're old enough to know better, and I do not meddle in things that are not my business. This is your room. And yours, Miss, is next to hers."

"Come see me when you're settled," Hyacinth whispered behind the landlady's broad back before disappearing into her room.

Mrs. Adams led Eliza to the next door. "I didn't catch your purpose in being in Remembrance."

You sly thing, Eliza thought, but she simply answered, "I used to live here."

"Davis is your name, correct? The only Davis family I remember left several years ago. Somebody got sick. The father?"

"No, my mother. We left here to get her medical treatment in St. Paul, but it wasn't successful. She passed away shortly after that." Eliza swallowed. How often was she going to have to relive this? There were undoubtedly people in Remembrance who knew her parents. She'd been only a child when she lived here and hadn't paid much attention to the adults, preferring to play with her dolls and cats. Plus, fifteen years of absence placed a blur over names and faces.

"I'm sorry to hear that." Mrs. Adams opened the door to Eliza's room. "This room will be yours."

She carried Eliza's bag in and placed it by the foot of the bed. Then she brushed her hand over the bureau, wiping away an invisible speck of dust, and said as she left, "Have a pleasant sleep. Breakfast at seven, church after eight."

Eliza surveyed her surroundings. This would be her new home for a while.

The room at the Mrs. Adams's Boardinghouse was clean, if a bit small. Next to her bed was a bright rag rug, its colorful scraps circling into a kaleidoscope of color. A white-painted nightstand was nearby, and Eliza smiled as she noticed the Bible centered squarely on the top. She could imagine Mrs. Adams placing it there, as if commanding the guest to read it.

She opened the carpetbag, and the clean scent of soap rose from it. One of the women she'd sewn for told her to tuck a cake of soap in her clothing and one in her carpetbag to keep her clothing smelling fresh, and she'd done so ever since. It was better than perfume.

She hung the few dresses she'd brought with her in the armoire, placed her toiletries on the bureau, and tucked her sewing kit in the top drawer of the chest. It was her prized possession—that bag with the assortment of needles and threads and the scissors that were kept knife-sharp. The kit had given her employment before, and it needed to again. She gave it one final tap before closing the drawer.

If only she'd been able to bring her sewing machine! She'd just gotten it a few months ago, but in her hurry to leave, she'd left it in the shop.

For a moment, she stood in the middle of the room.

She had done it. She had left St. Paul, left Blaine and his loathsome lies, and come back to Remembrance. Now, her life was going to start anew.

She already had a friend. Two, if she could count Silas, but she wasn't sure she could. He hadn't seemed happy to see them at the station—in fact, if she were a wagering woman she might bet that he'd have been happier if he'd gone to meet the train and they hadn't stepped off.

Still, he looked nice. He certainly didn't have the oily charm of Blaine—the thought almost made her laugh aloud as she recalled how ungraciously Silas had met them—but there was still something basically nice. He didn't seem comfortable being ungracious, maybe that was it.

Or perhaps she was trying to find something to like in somebody, anybody, to counteract the distress Blaine caused her.

Eliza wanted to freshen up a bit before visiting with Hyacinth, so she poured a bit of water from the pitcher over her hands and splashed it on her face. It was cold—of course—and invigorating.

She turned to the mirror, and what she saw there confirmed her worst fears. Four hours of traveling hadn't done her hair any favors. The braid that was wrapped into a knot at the back of her neck was still in place, but all around her face the shorter bits of hair had escaped, surrounding her head with a brown frizzy cloud that made her look as if she'd just woken up. The bow had come untied and straggled down the side of her neck in a trail of wrinkled blue velvet.

Great. Just great. Her first introduction to Remembrance and she looked totally disreputable.

She tried to slick her hair into place. Her hair had been the source of constant struggle since she was born. It was thick and curly and brown, not a pretty brown, she thought, but rather a floorboard brown. With all the wonderful things God could have topped her head with, why this? It was especially unfair here in Minnesota, where most women had Scandinavian hair, blonde and straight.

No, not blonde nor auburn nor even ebony black. Her hair was the color of wooden planks.

She gave up and went to Hyacinth's room.

"I thought perhaps you weren't coming," the older woman greeted her.

"I was lamenting my hair. You have such pretty hair, jet with ivory streaks." Eliza plopped on the chair.

Hyacinth laughed. "You make it sound so poetic. I like that. So, dear, what do you think of Remembrance so far? Is it at all what you expected?"

"I lived here so long ago," Eliza said honestly, "that what I expected was impossible. I know that the town couldn't stay the same way just because I left it, even if in my mind it was so."

"Well said. Tomorrow would you like to visit your old home again? We could explore together a bit after church."

"You'll want to spend that time with Edward. I can venture forth on my own. Somehow I don't think I'll get lost in Remembrance." A yawn took her by surprise. "Oh, I am so sorry! That came out of nowhere!"

"You get some sleep. We'll talk more tomorrow. Good night—and I'm glad I met you." Hyacinth gave her a quick hug. "Sweet dreams."

Back in her room, she began to unwind her disobedient hair, but her fingers were clumsy from lack of sleep. She hadn't realized until now just how tired she was, but as soon as she sank onto the bed to remove her shoes, the urge to put her head atop the pillow, on the crisp white case edged with green crocheted lace, and pull the green-spotted quilt over her head was nearly irresistible. She fought the fatigue and managed her before-bed rituals, slipping on a white cotton nightgown and hurrying under the covers.

She thought of the Bible as she gave in to her exhaustion, but her hands wouldn't—no, couldn't—make another motion. Instead, she began to recite the Twenty-Third Psalm from memory, her lips moving as she breathed the words that had always been such comfort. "The Lord is my shepherd; I shall not want. He maketh me to lie down. . ."

Eliza smiled. That was true. It might be a green quilt rather than a green pasture, but already her soul was feeling better.

Every muscle in her body screamed for sleep. Her nerves were stretched as far as they could go, but even the psalm couldn't bring the respite she needed. No matter what she tried, she could not sleep. Her body was ready, but her brain was still wide-awake.

She got out of the bed and dug into her satchel until she found the blue knit slippers she'd brought. At one point, she'd planned them for her trousseau, but that dream withered just hours ago, when she saw Blaine Loring with the other woman.

Now they were simply slippers to keep her feet warm against the cold.

She padded to the window. The snow cover reflected the partial moonlight, brightening the darkness. The snow had tapered off, with only a few scattered flakes gliding slowly through the air.

From her vantage point on the second floor, she could see Remembrance laid out below her. It looked peaceful, serene. It had changed so much since she'd left. How old was she then? Nine? Ten? Her father packed them up and moved them to St. Paul, searching for the ever-elusive cure for her mother's illness. When she'd died two months later, he began searching for a home for his soul, moving with his daughter again and again until he gave up and breathed his last. He was buried in St. Paul, next to his beloved wife.

Eliza put her head down on the chilly windowsill and let the pain wash over her. It was so unfair. She'd lost everything she loved, everyone she loved.

Someday she would cry about it all. Someday. Right now she needed to step back and study her life, to see if she could determine God's promised path. It was there. She couldn't see it now, but it was there.

A huge yawn overtook her. Whatever God meant for her future, it was going to have to wait. Right now He wanted her to get some sleep.

As she stood up, a figure moved, a dark silhouette against the whitened backdrop of the new snowfall. The man walked along the town square, his footprints showing gray in the snow. Around he went, until at last he turned toward the line of houses lining the street and vanished around the corner.

Could it be Silas, out for a late evening stroll? She shivered and scurried toward the warmth of the bed. Some people might enjoy a winter night in Minnesota, but not her—at least not when she was this desperately tired.

She slid into the bed and dutifully prayed her bedtime verse that she had ended each day with for as long as she could remember. "Thank You for Your gifts I pray, thank You for this special day, for the morning light and the evening star, and bless those who love us near and far."

❧

The morning light spilled into the kitchen of the Collier house. Silas poured a cup of coffee and took it into the parlor. He'd rebuilt the fire in the stove, and the bright flames were taking the chill off the start of the day. His coat had fallen from the hook by the door. He must have hung it too hastily when he returned last night. Four times around the town square, trying to think through what couldn't be thought through, and then trying to rid his mind of the topic entirely.

It'd been a fool's errand.

Sunday mornings were special. He liked the slow start, the quiet hours that preceded the church service.

Now maybe things would change. He shook his head. No, there was no *maybe* about it. Things would change.

He sipped the coffee, staring out the window. From where he stood, he could see the edge of the boardinghouse. There were two women there who were about to turn his life topsy-turvy. He knew what Hyacinth's role would be—but what about Eliza's? There was something about her that intrigued him.

He shrugged. There was no use in overthinking this. He'd make better use of his time getting ready for church.

He made it to the top stair when his uncle called out from his bedroom. "Silas!"

He opened the door and looked in. "Are you feeling all right? Does your ankle hurt? I told you that you shouldn't have gone to the train station with me last night."

Uncle Edward waved away his question. "*Pfft*. It's just a bone. I would have walked through hot lava to see her at long last. Isn't she wonderful?" He smiled dreamily.

Silas didn't answer right away. On one hand, he had some doubts—no, cancel that, he had a whole wagonful of doubts—about someone who would move to be near someone she hadn't even met, someone she might, in fact, marry.

On the other hand, he had enough respect for his uncle not to willingly hurt his feelings, so he didn't want to blurt out his true feelings.

And on still another hand—he chuckled slightly at the realization he had three hands going in this internal argument—he was not about to lie. He didn't like falsehoods, and lying on a Sunday seemed especially dreadful.

At last he settled for a noncommittal and truthful, "She seems quite interesting."

His uncle boosted himself up straighter in the bed. "Say, did I hear you leave last night? Were you out for a late night stroll?"

"Yes, sir. My legs needed some stretching." It wasn't a lie. It felt wonderful to go for a walk and let his muscles get some exercise.

"I know what you mean, son. If it weren't for this cracked-up leg, I might have joined you." Edward sat up, carefully maneuvering his swaddled ankle around the blankets. "Hyacinth is quite a woman, isn't she?"

He did not want to talk about it. This woman was the cause of everything that had gone wrong. If it hadn't been for Hyacinth, Uncle Edward wouldn't have been renovating a perfectly good house. He wouldn't have decided to put up that ridiculous plaster bouquet on the door, and he certainly wouldn't have let himself lose his balance and fall off the ladder and break his ankle.

He knew that men did the most ridiculous things for women. Not him, though. He'd keep his head—or better still, never fall in love to begin with. What a silly notion it was. Why, Professor Barkley advised great control in matters of the heart.

Unfortunately, his uncle was not a student of Professor Barkley and fell headfirst into this middle-aged amour.

But the fact of the matter was that what had happened had happened and wasn't about to un-happen. So he smiled at Uncle Edward. "Indeed."

"I'm going to church with you," his uncle announced, swinging his legs over the side of the bed and grimacing.

"Are you sure that's a good idea?" Silas frowned. "We got a good snow last night. You shouldn't even have gone last night to the station."

Uncle Edward shot him a look that brooked no argument. "I am going to church, and I am going to sit with my beloved."

"Well," Silas said, "let's get you up and presentable because I do believe that your beloved won't want you until you've shaved and washed." He grinned. "And changed out of your nightshirt."

Soon the two of them were headed for the church, Silas walking slowly beside his uncle in case he slipped. Luckily the church was just around the corner, but still the trip seemed to take forever.

Down the road they could see the two boarders from Mrs. Adams's house heading toward church, with Mrs. Adams herself leading the way like a plump mother hen.

He smiled as he noticed Eliza and Hyacinth trailing immediately behind the matronly woman, no more than an arm's reach away from the landlady. He knew that Mrs. Adams put them there to make sure they approached the house of worship with the proper decorum.

His uncle stepped forward, sliding a bit on the icy step in the entrance of the church. Silas caught him before he could fall. "Careful," he warned, but Uncle Edward ignored him.

"Hyacinth, dear!" he called. "Lambkins!"

If only there were a hole nearby, he could sink into it, Silas thought. His uncle had clearly gone around the bend mentally. If he were going to be acting like a love-stricken fool, the least he could do was behave that way in the privacy of his own home, not out in the public like this—and definitely not while Silas was standing beside him.

Hyacinth waved enthusiastically. "Darling!"

He couldn't help it. He looked at Eliza, who was, to his horror, gazing straight at him, a smile dimpling her cheeks with humor. Mentally he consulted with Professor Barkley— and drew a blank. If the good teacher dealt with such issues, it must be later on in the course of study.

Expect the unexpected. That one had been last week, and was perhaps applicable for this situation. It struck him as odd when he'd read it then, and now, when the time came to put Professor Barkley's principle into action, it fell short. How could he expect the unexpected? If he could expect it, it wouldn't be unexpected.

Furthermore, Professor Barkley urged him to prepare for the unexpected so that when it did come his way, he'd be ready for it. Silas snorted to himself. Hardly possible!

Eliza came up the walk to the church's entrance, avoiding the reunion of Edward and Hyacinth. He automatically reached out to help her across the icy spot where his uncle had almost lost his bearings, and the sight of her small, gloved hand against the woolen cloth of his overcoat did something odd to his knees.

Professor Barkley had clearly never dealt with a female hand on his coat, or he would have made that the first chapter of his book.

A little part of him that was rampantly vain was pleased

that he'd worn his good overcoat this morning rather than the buffalo robe, which could get quite pungent in close quarters.

A group of children clattered in front of them, while a man with sunken and bloodshot eyes tried ineffectively to round them up.

"Good morning, Jack," Silas said to him, nabbing a young boy as he raced by and slinging him to his shoulder. "Here, I've got Mark."

"Thanks, Silas. All right, children, we are in God's house. Let's be worshipful," Jack said to his children.

Each child, from the oldest to the youngest, put their hands together and walked reverently down the aisle.

"That's Jack Robbins," Silas whispered. "Poor fellow has his hands full, that's for sure, what with six children and a wife who's been sick all winter. He's a good man, and makes sure his children get to church each Sunday."

"I remember him! They lived on the other side of Remembrance, and he was older than I was, maybe three or four years ahead of me in school, but I recall that he was kind and helped the younger children who had trouble understanding their sums."

"You remember him?" Silas asked, stopping so suddenly that Eliza nearly tripped. "I didn't realize you had ever lived here in Remembrance."

"That was fifteen years ago. I don't remember much about it, to be honest. Your uncle looks a bit familiar, but I don't recall Mrs. Adams, who says she knew my parents. I was just a child." She laughed softly. "Somehow grown-ups weren't nearly as important as my cats."

Silas tapped his uncle on the shoulder. "Miss Davis here used to live in Remembrance. Did you know that?"

Edward turned to her slowly, obviously reluctant to take his gaze off his new love. "Oh, that's very nice."

Silas rolled his eyes. There was clearly going to be no talking to his uncle until the man came to his senses—*if* he came to his senses.

So Eliza had lived in Remembrance before and had come back. He asked the question that arose naturally. "Are you going to stay here?"

"Perhaps," she responded lightly. He was unable to pursue the matter further as Reverend Tupper began the call to worship, and they hurried to their seats.

The four of them—Silas, Eliza, Hyacinth, and Edward— sat together during the service. As soon as Reverend Tupper announced the Gospel for the day, Silas squirmed. Matthew 22 was the parable of the wedding feast.

Why couldn't the minister have chosen something else? Lepers or wars or burning bushes would have been good. Why the wedding feast?

The rosy-cheeked minister, as short and round as a pumpkin, described the wedding feast. To Silas's right, Uncle Edward and Hyacinth beamed at each other happily. He glanced surreptitiously at Eliza. She looked ahead, her gaze steadily on Reverend Tupper.

Silas didn't want to hear about a wedding feast, or anything else to do with weddings. Out of the corner of his eye, he saw Edward reach for Hyacinth's hand. This was getting worse.

He'd hoped that his uncle would see the light of reality and come to his senses. How could a grown man, usually so stalwart and intelligent, fall in love through a series of letters?

He didn't like being embarrassed by Edward's behavior, either. Life was hard enough as it was, without being plagued by something so totally out of his control. Maybe, he considered with a quick hope, his uncle had some kind of dementia that led him to this foolish relationship.

The minister reminded the congregation that the parable was about the kingdom of God. He leaned forward, his face beaming with the joy of his message, as he exhorted them to come to the banquet.

Then, with his usual good humor, he ended the service by noting that dinner with pie and coffee would be served by the Women's League. "Different banquet, same theory. Please choose to come," he quipped.

The back of the church had been turned into a temporary dining room. As usual, the other members of the congregation served the Robbins children first, and Silas caught the littlest boy's wobbling plate before it slipped to the floor. "Do you do this every week?" Eliza asked Silas as she accepted a dish heaped with ham and beans.

"In the summer it's easier. We sit outside. We try to do it every week, yes. There's a very active Women's League." He glanced over at Hyacinth and his uncle, bent over a plate. "Mrs. Mason will have to join."

"Have to join? You make it sound like it's a requirement."

"It is, in a way. This church was built with great enthusiasm and optimism. You'll note that it seats about one hundred and seventy people. One hundred and eighty if they're family." He grinned. "But at the moment, there are only one hundred people or so in Remembrance proper, and that includes the very old and the very young and a few dogs and cats. The church needs everyone participating."

"Including Hyacinth."

He didn't want to argue the point, and in fact, he wasn't sure that she did, either. He speared a piece of ham, stuck it in his mouth, and chewed thoughtfully. He wanted to answer her as honestly as possible. "They'll take to her like barn swallows to the wind, as my father used to say. You know that saying, 'Many hands make light work'? Well, it's true. The more people who pitch in, the better the outcome. Anyone who volunteers to help in any capacity is welcome here. Plus she'll make friends in the Women's League. Good friends."

"That's true." Eliza seemed to understand what he was saying, which oddly mattered to him—quite a bit.

Reverend Tupper joined them and introduced himself. "I hope you'll be with us quite a while," he said to Eliza.

"I'm enjoying my time here," she said, rather neatly avoiding a direct answer, Silas noted.

"And how did you come to choose Remembrance?" the minister continued.

"Remembrance chose me, I'd say," she responded with a smile. "I lived here when I was a child, but my parents and I moved to St. Paul when my mother became ill. It was quite awhile ago, and both of my parents have passed on now, but I was ready to see what became of Remembrance."

Silas realized he was as anxious to hear more as the minister was.

Reverend Tupper began to speak, but another parishioner tugged at his elbow with a request about the stove. "We'll discuss more later, I do hope," he finished.

"I'm sure we will," she answered.

"He's a bit inquisitive," Silas told her as he handed his empty plate to one of the women at the table and took up the piece of apple pie she handed him, "but it's to his advantage. He knows his flock as well as any good shepherd."

"Oh, I don't deny him that," she said, "and in fact, I'd have liked to have visited with him some more. I wanted to ask him about the Gospel reading he used."

"The wedding banquet story? What was your question?"

"I always felt bad for the guest who didn't have the right clothes," Eliza said. "I know it's a parable, but to be thrown out simply because he wasn't dressed appropriately—doesn't that seem a bit harsh?"

Her question caught him off guard. "Harsh? I hadn't thought about it. But if you're invited to a wedding by a king, wouldn't you wear your finest?"

"What if it were his finest?" she persisted.

"Well," Silas hedged, aware that he was well out of his theological waters, "the Bible does say that the man was supposed to have worn his wedding garment, not that I'm at all sure what a wedding garment would have been in that time. . ."

She laughed. "I imagine I take it a bit more literally than most, being a dressmaker."

"Truly? You're a dressmaker? Why then, would you come to Remembrance? Oh, I know what you said to Reverend Tupper, but wouldn't you have more business in St. Paul?"

Was he mistaken, or did her expression falter? "My business was prospering in St. Paul, but I was drawn to a smaller community, a closer community, like Remembrance. I have good memories of living here, even if they're a bit faded and dusty themselves."

He led her to two chairs that had become vacant when the occupants left the church. "Did you not enjoy St. Paul? I'd think a city would be exciting."

She shrugged, but he saw a flash of something—pain?—across her face. "Exciting? Oh, yes. It was very exciting, but I got to the point where I was abandoning my upbringing and turning my back on God." Again, the flicker of hurt flared in her eyes. "I lost the person I was, and I knew I needed to regain her. That is why I returned to Remembrance."

He touched her arm, his large hand on her pale blue sleeve, and he was again struck by the comparison of the earlier image of her delicate hand on his overcoat. She was so small that he felt like a lumbering giant next to her.

"I'm glad you did."

three

A knock on Eliza's door was followed by, "Eliza, dear, are you ready to go?"

She practically flew to the door to let Hyacinth in. "I am. Did you talk to Mrs. Adams about our going to supper at the Collier house? What did she say?"

"Of course she was a bit put out since she'd already planned the meal, although our saving grace was that she hadn't actually prepared it yet.

"By the way, Eliza, she has her ideas of what ladies do and what gentlemen do and what courting is all about and—"

"Courting? Courting? Who's courting me? Silas? Oh, honestly!" Eliza shook her head with exasperation.

Hyacinth sat on the edge of the bed and pulled Eliza down beside her. "It sounds strange to you, and yes, to me, too, but we have to remember where we are. You're not living on your own in St. Paul anymore, and I'm not in Chicago."

"I can take care of myself," Eliza protested.

"You can, of course." Hyacinth's words were soothing. "As can I. We both know that.

"But the fact is that we need to be a bit inconspicuous at first. Not, of course," she hurriedly added, "that either of us has anything to be ashamed of."

Eliza looked down. She wasn't ready yet to tell anyone the soil upon her life.

"Have you ever had a cat, Eliza?"

She snapped her head up. What on earth was the woman

37

talking about? "Yes, I've had a cat."

"How many?"

"I had one. His name was Tim. And then I got another one, Hannah."

"But Tim was first, right? And then Hannah?"

"Yes, but I don't see—" Eliza drummed her fingertips silently on the quilt. What did this have to do with Mrs. Adams?

"Hear me out. How did Hannah react when she came to the house? How did she treat Tim?"

"She was very quiet and hid most of the time, and then slowly she came out from under the bed and behind the couch and sat with us, until she and Tim were the best of friends—oh! I see!"

"Exactly," Hyacinth said as she stood up. "Hannah fit in by lying low and not fighting with Tim. That gave Tim the time that he needed to get to know her, and it let Hannah figure out what was what. It made the adjustment as painless as possible."

"So that's what we need to do?" Eliza asked. "We need to be Hannah to Mrs. Adams's Tim."

"That's one way to put it," Hyacinth said, with a smile. "For the moment, unless our landlady—or anyone—becomes totally outrageous, we'll abide by the rules. They're strict, I'll give you that, but not without reason, I'm sure."

Her advice made sense. Yet, Eliza thought as they left the boardinghouse with Mrs. Adams's frowning face watching them from the window, it was a bit too much. Well, she thought philosophically, she could try. It wasn't as if she'd live in the boardinghouse forever.

There wasn't a cloud in the sky, and the air was icily crisp. Eliza tugged her scarf up tighter around her face, and then dug her hands into the muff she'd brought along. With no wind to lash at their faces, this was the perfect day to explore a wintry Remembrance.

"Do you remember where you lived?" Hyacinth asked as they headed to their right.

"I thought I did, but it feels like somebody rearranged all the houses. I was sure it was down this road, but these other homes weren't here so everything looks different. I'm not sure."

For fifteen years, she'd built the town in her mind, and rebuilt it and rebuilt it. It was the home where she went in her dreams, it was the place she fled to in her memory when she was feeling alone, it was the solace she sought when her soul ached. She knew exactly what it looked like, right down to the snow-covered branches outside the church.

"We can find it, I'm sure," Hyacinth declared. "We'll wander until we do. How long can it take us, anyway? Remembrance isn't that big."

The town had changed much, but the core was still essentially the same, Eliza realized as they walked along the snow-packed roads, stopping only to exclaim over a bright blue doorway or a stained-glass transom. There was a pride evident in Remembrance, a sense of community that she had been too young to notice as a child, but which she saw in the tender care the Robbins family received at the church.

"This is it."

There, in front of her, was the house she and her parents had lived in. In many ways, it hadn't changed much. The clapboards were white and the shutters were black, and the red flower boxes were still in the front.

In other ways, though, it was completely transformed. She and her father left with the house wrapped in the dark specter of illness. The rooms themselves hung heavy with sadness. Now it seemed to sparkle with renewed life. Signs of children were obvious: a wagon abandoned near a bush and filled with snow, a doll propped in one window and a cloth dog in another. A room had been added to the side, and bushes had been planted on each side of the front door.

"How are you feeling?" Hyacinth asked softly.

Eliza shook her head. "I don't know. Not bad, I know that. I was so heartbroken when we left here. I think we both knew that my mother wouldn't live, but there was that glimmer of hope that maybe a doctor in the city could save her, and we chased that hope. I'm glad to see that the house isn't so depressed—oh, now I'm being silly. How can a house be depressed?"

Hyacinth shrugged. "That probably falls under the heading of 'mysterious ways.' I imagine that, at the very least, when your mother was so ill, when you knew she was dying, you saw things differently. I know that's what happened when my Matthew passed on. I felt as if God threw a black veil over everything. Nothing looked the same, nothing smelled the same, nothing tasted the same."

Her words shot Eliza back into the past, into the days of pain. Losing her father was still a raw grief, too. "Exactly."

She was suddenly transported back to Remembrance fifteen years ago. It was the start of a summer filled with promise. Eliza had loved summer, loved the juicy strawberries, the sweet corn, the little fish that nibbled on her feet when she waded in the river.

And then her mother got very sick. Days and nights were indistinguishable, as the curtained windows blocked out any bit of sunshine that her mother might have found painful. It happened so quickly that it seemed like a dream, one that she'd wake up from and her mother would be well and they'd be on their way to the berry patch to get the best selection before the birds got there.

The fever stole not only her mother but it also snatched away her father's smile and stripped her young life of joy.

Tears burned at her eyelids as the horrible pain returned full force, undiluted by the years. She missed her mother desperately, grieved for her father anew.

They began to walk on. "I felt as if my heart had been slashed by a great knife. It hurt so bad, as a matter of fact, that I thought I was dying, too, and I actually went to the doctor. He said that yes, I was sick—heartsick—and the only way to recover was to grieve Matthew with my whole being and move on."

"That seems a bit, I don't know, callous," Eliza ventured.

"Not really, although at the time I thought he was horrible to even suggest such a thing. No, I must say that I've never forgotten Matthew. Never. I also had to forgive him for dying—and come to terms with the fact that God took him from me."

"How did you do that?" Eliza found herself clinging to every word. "Did you forgive God?"

Hyacinth laughed. "Oh, my dear, one doesn't forgive God! We can understand Him a bit more, but I wouldn't call it 'forgiving.' I wish Matthew hadn't died, but he did, and now it's time for me to let myself love again."

"And that's why you're in Remembrance."

"That's right. Edward and I have a mutual friend who thought we'd enjoy each other's company. He introduced us by a letter, and Edward and I took it from there. I came to love him so much." Hyacinth's face grew soft. "He is a good man."

"But what about Matthew? How can you love twice?"

Hyacinth put her arm around Eliza. "That is the most

astonishing thing. God created this fragile thing called a heart, and then gave it the most amazing ability—the capacity for love that expands as needed."

"But hearts can be wounded. And sometimes they don't recover." She thought of her father, who never healed from his beloved wife's death.

"There's the mystery—because sometimes they do. Sometimes they do."

Eliza pondered what Hyacinth said. Her own heart had been pounded terribly, and letting herself love again was too great a risk.

Oh, she was simply being silly. Moving to Remembrance had pretty much taken care of that danger. How many eligible men were even available? This was a small town, after all.

❧

They were about to complete their survey of Remembrance, having come nearly full circle in their tour, when Hyacinth pointed out a small house behind the mercantile. "If I remember correctly, this is the house I'll be renting. Let's go peek in the windows."

"Are you sure we can? What if it isn't the right place?" Eliza asked nervously.

"Oh, I'm sure it's right. Edward described it well enough in the letters. He said it had a birdbath in the front, and do you see any others with a birdbath? And he said it was behind the store, and this is. And it certainly looks empty."

Eliza trailed after Hyacinth. She'd feel a bit better if she knew for sure—

A small body cannonballed into her. "Got you!" the reedy voice shouted as the boy's arms wrapped around her legs.

She recognized one of the Robbins boys. He couldn't have been more than six years old. "You startled me!" she said, snatching off his knit cap and ruffling his hair. "What are you doing?"

The boy took the cap back and shoved it on his head. "I'm protecting this for Mr. Collier," he said, throwing his chest out proudly. "He asked me to keep an eye on it, and I am."

Eliza knelt in front of the child. "Do you know why? Because Mrs. Mason here is going to move into it."

"Oh." His face sagged. "I'm so sorry, ladies. I thought you might be robbers."

"Well, we could have been," Hyacinth said, joining them. "You were certainly Johnny-on-the-spot with paying attention, too."

"My name's not Johnny. It's Paul."

"I see." Eliza fought back a smile. He was so serious. "I'm glad to meet you, Paul. I believe I saw you in church this morning."

"Yes, ma'am, I was there. Say, I'm sorry I tackled you like that. Do you think Mr. Collier will be mad at me?"

"You did a good job, Paul," Eliza said. "And no, he won't be angry. If anything, he'll be proud of how vigilant you were."

"You must live near here," Hyacinth said.

"Yes, ma'am." He pointed to a house two lots down. "You should come visit us sometime."

"We will," Eliza said, rising to her feet and brushing the snow off the front of her coat. "We'll see you again soon!"

As they walked toward the Collier house, they chuckled over the little boy's solemn caretaking of the house. "At least I know I'll be safe when I live there," Hyacinth said.

Edward and Silas lived on the other side of the town square. The air held the January thaw warmth, but as the evening shadows overtook their footsteps, a definite chill invaded the day's moderate temperatures.

The Collier house looked much like the others on the street, "tall and thin," as Hyacinth described it, built to take advantage of the fact that heat would rise in the cold winter months, thus warming the upper story a bit more.

Silas met them at the door, with Edward peering over his shoulder, his excitement nearly palpable.

Something utterly delicious scented the air. "I hope you both like chicken pie," Silas said as he took their coats. "Uncle Edward is a talented cook."

"But he's using a crutch!" Hyacinth objected, scurrying into the kitchen.

Silas looked at Eliza, and they chorused softly, "His precious limb!"

"I suspect they'll be in there a bit, finishing up the dinner, and fussing over each other," Silas said, "so let's sit in here."

The front room was small but neat. A grandfather clock ticked in the corner, and the fireplace crackled as a log fell.

Near the fireplace were two chairs covered in slick damask. Eliza sat in one and had to grip the arms to keep seated on the stiff cushion. "One of Uncle Edward's projects to prepare for Hyacinth," he said as he sat in the other chair. Eliza noticed that he, too, held onto the arms. "New upholstery. He's sure they'll become more comfortable as time goes on."

I should certainly hope so! Eliza thought, but aloud she merely said, "They will get broken in soon enough."

Most of the furnishings in the room did seem new or refurbished, and even the ruinous plaster molding of a bouquet of flowers had been successfully nailed in place, undoubtedly the work of the more-focused Silas.

"The house is truly finished beautifully," Eliza said. "I understand that you and your uncle both have excellent carpentry skills." Mrs. Adams had filled her in on that. "Have you always been interested in woodworking?"

"It's something my uncle and I share." Silas stared contemplatively into the fire. "I grew up near Crookston—do you know where that is?"

She nodded. Much larger than Remembrance, Crookston was near the border of the Dakota Territory.

"My family moved back to Pennsylvania when I was thirteen, and instead of going with them, I came here, to apprentice with Uncle Edward."

This would explain why she and Silas hadn't met when she'd lived here. He didn't arrive until several years after she'd moved away.

"Did you want to be a carpenter?"

He looked directly at her with clear surprise. "What an odd question."

"One that's worth asking, I believe."

For a moment, he didn't answer. Then he replied, "I was thirteen. All I knew was that I didn't want to move to Pennsylvania. My father was planning to take over his father's printing company, and I couldn't think of anything more dreadful than that."

She chuckled. "Ah, the unerring wisdom of youth."

"Truly. Uncle Edward offered to take me and teach me woodworking, and it was here in this house and in the shop in the back that I found my calling. Carpentry is—well, let's just say that he taught me well."

"Then this time has worked out for both of you."

He shrugged. "According to my uncle, I have a talent for wood. Of course, he could be saying that only because I'm his nephew."

"Or he could be saying it because it's true."

He took off his glasses and cleaned them carefully, even

though Eliza suspected there wasn't a spot on them. Silas didn't seem to be the kind to appreciate compliments.

"Whatever his reason, I'm here and I'm now a carpenter. Life has a way of changing when you least expect it."

"That's a good way of looking at it," Eliza said. He had no way of knowing how applicable his words were to her life, too. "Then you're staying on to work with your uncle?"

His lips tightened slightly. "I don't believe so. Remembrance is a small town, and there really isn't a need for two carpenters here."

"But if Hyacinth stays—"

"But if Hyacinth stays, my uncle will need to retain the business. Having another person in the household—" He broke off before he could finish what he was saying, but she understood. The problem was one facing all the small towns that were starting up: finding an income that would support a family, no matter how large or how small.

"Reverend Tupper has asked me to talk about something with you," he said, suddenly changing subjects. "There's a family in Remembrance who has fallen on some hard times. You saw the father and his children today in church. Jack Robbins is the fellow's name."

"Ah, yes." Eliza told him, in light words, of their encounter with Paul.

"Yes," Silas said with a slight smile. "Paul is very responsible. I'll have to tell him how much I appreciate his apprehension of the possible criminals today. He's a good child, but in danger of being old beyond his years."

He told her more of the situation at the Robbins house. Mary Robbins was quite ill, and Jack was having to let his own work drop to care for her and their family.

"That can be quite difficult," she said, thinking back to her own childhood and the similar circumstances she lived with.

"Indeed it can. The church is helping as best it can, and Reverend Tupper has inquired if you might be able to help with some of your needlework skills. The older women in the church can—and have—done quite a bit, but there is much more." Silas sighed. "There are six children in the family, and they're growing so very quickly."

"As children are wont to do."

"True. I'm going in this next week to do some repairs in the house. Might you—"

"Yes."

"You will?" The relief in his voice was clear. "That's wonderful!"

At that moment, the door to the kitchen burst open, and Hyacinth ran out, a smoking pan in her hands. "Coming through!" she sang as she raced across the room and out the front door. Within seconds she returned, without the pan in her hands, but her eyes were twinkling. "We won't be having turnips tonight."

Edward's face peeked around the corner of the door, and he grinned.

"I am not going to ask what that was about," Silas said. "Eliza, I do believe we'd better head toward the dining room before the rest of the dinner goes up in flames."

~

The dinner, which Silas had been dreading, passed, and he actually enjoyed it. He could have managed nicely without Uncle Edward pointing out how well Silas and Eliza were getting along, how their friendship was blossoming, how they'd be working together for the Robbins family, even how they both liked chicken pie. He'd stopped short of carving their initials in the tree by the front door.

Now Eliza and Hyacinth had gone back to Mrs. Adams, and Uncle Edward was inside, puttering around and setting things back in order, while Silas stood in the winter moonlight.

But things couldn't go back into order. Not now.

A snowflake fell on his cheek, and then another and another. He looked at the moon in the cloudless sky. When he was little, he thought that God lived there, so far away, but he came to know over the years that He was never further than Silas's thoughts.

He'd only known Eliza for twenty-four hours, and while he was not a believer in love at first sight, he did believe in the power of friendship, and that's exactly what he was labeling this as. Hadn't Professor Barkley himself endorsed friendship?

Maybe he needed a friend, and that's what he was finding in Eliza. He hadn't had anyone he could consider a friend—someone to laugh with, someone to share secret jokes with. Someone who found "precious limb" as funny as he did.

A gust of wind whipped around the edge of the house, and he shivered. It was time to go back inside and put this day to rest.

Uncle Edward had finished his final touches in the kitchen and was hobbling up the stairs, one awkward step at a time. Silas rushed to his rescue.

"Why don't you let me fix a bed downstairs," he said, "so you don't have to do this every night?"

His uncle shook his head. "There's nothing like a fellow's own bed. Just lead me to it. I know I've got some sweet dreams ahead of me." He winked at Silas. "You, too, I suspect."

"Humph. I'll be dreaming of turnips that someone managed to burn, that's what I'll be dreaming about. That smell will take weeks to go away."

"You think I did it because I don't like turnips, don't you?"

Silas grinned. "Maybe."

"There are some things that are more important than turnips, Silas. Love is."

Silas patted his uncle on the shoulder. "That's true. Now get some sleep."

In the haven of his own room, Silas eagerly turned to the day's lesson in *Professor Barkley's Patented Five Year Plan for Success*. Sunday, he read, was meant to be a day of rest and reflection. And how did a man do that? Planning ahead, Professor Barkley counseled. Prepare for the Holy Day by gathering your clothes, cooking your food in advance, and laying out the items you would need so they would be at hand.

Planning ahead? Professor Barkley should try living in this house.

The lesson also included the admonition to read the Good Book daily and to commit a Bible verse to memory each day.

Silas's eyes threatened to shut before he could finish the day's directive, but he forced himself to read on. The recommended verse for him to learn was John 8:32: *And ye shall know the truth, and the truth shall make you free.*

Easy. Easy to memorize, easy to understand.

He ran through his evening prayer and slid under the covers.

The truth. It was easy. . .wasn't it?

four

Eliza tucked the last strand of hair into the bun coiled at the nape of her neck. Trying to make it stay was a losing battle, but if she didn't turn too quickly, and if she was careful removing her knit scarf, the lock might stay in place.

As if to taunt her, the wayward strand immediately slid out, but before she could do battle with it again, someone knocked on her door. She abandoned the tussle with her hair and opened the door.

Mrs. Adams stood there, her arms crossed over her calicoed chest. "Silas Collier is downstairs. He said he'll walk with you over to the church."

"Good. Thank you for letting me know. I'll be right down." Eliza reached for her coat, but Mrs. Adams didn't move. Obviously she had more to say. Eliza suppressed a smile. Mrs. Adams always had more to say.

"He didn't tell me, but I heard at the market this morning that you have volunteered to help the Robbins family out." The crusty demeanor softened. "Thank you."

Then the grumpy bearing was right back in place. "Don't forget. Dinner is at noon. Prompt. I don't hold the food for anybody."

"Thank you so much, I will remember."

"You've got a bit of hair that's gone awry," Mrs. Adams commented, as if the lock had itself violated one of her many rules. Perhaps reassuring herself that her own steely gray hair was safely confined within the limits of the braided circle at the nape of her neck, she ran her hand over the sides of the constrained hair. She smiled, maybe a bit smugly, Eliza thought, as her fingers found no stray tresses.

Eliza tucked the errant strand back into place and snatched up her coat and her sewing bag. "Thank you, Mrs. Adams. I don't know if I'll be back for dinner at noon or not. Silas and I are meeting Reverend Tupper in the church first." She paused. Should she ask? "I'm not quite sure what to expect when I get over to the Robbins's home."

"Expect a mess," the woman said succinctly. "The family needs help."

Mrs. Adams, Eliza had already found out, was more than willing to share what she knew. Perhaps she could give her some more information about what to expect at the Robbins's house.

"How long has Mrs. Robbins been ill?" Eliza asked.

"Several months, but when she fell ill, it was quick and terrible. Most of us didn't expect her to survive, to tell you the truth. She was very close to death's door." Mrs. Adams shook her head sadly.

Memories of her own mother's illness made Eliza's stomach clench. "But Mrs. Robbins is getting better, isn't she?"

Mrs. Adams didn't answer immediately, as if considering her answer. "She's alive," she said at last. "She's alive."

They left the room, and Eliza followed Mrs. Adams's heavy tread down the stairs.

"Silas is in the parlor," Mrs. Adams said, "waiting for you."

He rose when she entered the parlor, Mrs. Adams trailing closely behind her. "Just a minute." The older woman suddenly turned and bustled out of the room.

"What was that about?" Eliza asked as Silas helped her into her coat. "That woman has more surprises than Christmas."

"I have no idea," he answered.

Mrs. Adams returned quickly, a basket in her hands. It was covered with a large white napkin, neatly tucked in around the edges. She held it out to Silas. "Here. It should feed the lot of you."

As he took it from her, the warm aroma of baked turkey arose from it. "Mrs. Adams, you want me to take this with me?" he asked.

"Why else would I have given it to you?" she answered with a sniff. "It certainly seems obvious that your work crew would get a lot more done, and the Robbins family might have a decent meal, if you ate this over there."

"This is what you were going to serve for dinner today, isn't it?" Eliza asked, finally catching on to what Mrs. Adams had done. "What a wonderfully sweet thing to do!"

"Sweet? Well." Mrs. Adams seemed taken aback, as if no one had called her *sweet* in a long time—if ever. "I can make another dinner. Not turkey, mind you, but I can put together a nice potato and ham hot dish in its place. Mrs. Mason and I will enjoy that just as much."

"The family will certainly enjoy this. Thank you, Mrs. Adams," Silas said. "Eliza, we need to go."

The temperature had dropped overnight, and the wind had picked up. Conversation was impossible as Eliza tucked her chin deep inside her knitted scarf, covering as much of her face as she could with it. The wind was bitter, tugging at her skirts until they whipped around her ankles tightly.

The warmth of the church was welcome. Reverend Tupper had a small fire burning in the iron stove at the front of the church, and she held her hands out toward the flames.

"Thank you for sharing your talents with the family," he said to Eliza, who could only chatter wordlessly in response, her face was so frozen. "The Robbins house is not far away, but I'll give you a chance to thaw out a bit first. Silas, might I borrow you for a moment? I'd like you to look at the back window. . . ."

Their voices grew fainter as they walked away from her. Eliza huddled near the stove, letting the heat radiate into her body. It wasn't far to walk, but the wind was brutal, making every foot seem like a mile.

She looked around the church. When she'd lived here, the church had been smaller, not much larger than some of the original houses the settlers built. The community added onto it, even expanding the sanctuary. She ran her hand over the altar, undoubtedly crafted by one of townsmen, perhaps Edward or Silas even. It was smooth and polished, and ornamented with an iron cross centered on a white cloth, the edges touched with lace.

In a low murmur from the back of the church, she could hear the men's voices.

What an odd journey this had been. Within a week, she abandoned the life she'd been building—she'd *thought* she'd been building, she corrected herself—and had come back, full circle, to where she began.

It surprised her at first that no one seemed to recognize her name—no one except Mrs. Adams, of course—but she'd already realized that many people came to and left Remembrance, not having found the financial relief they'd been expecting here. Her family had been one in a steady stream of temporary residents.

In her memory, Remembrance staged itself as larger and grander, but in retrospect, she had to admit that nostalgia had put a gleam on the little town that was her own creation. It was, simply, the place she had been happiest.

Here her mother had been well, here her father had laughed, here she had played in the grass of the prairie.

But it had all been fleeting. When they left, they took everything. Her father emptied the house of its furniture and its quilts and its pictures, and sold it and the parcel of land it sat on to the next man ready to believe the promises of this new town in the north of the state. Now the woods surrounding it had become fields, and in time, the fields would become towns, more towns like Remembrance. Some would survive. Some wouldn't.

From the corner where the men spoke, she heard laughter. It was like music. There hadn't been much laughter with Blaine Loring. He was an intense man. It was, as he told her patiently one day, how he became wealthy. His single-focus approach to whatever he was doing meant that his project succeeded, but it also meant that there were casualties along the way. But he never concerned himself with that.

If she had paid attention to his words then, she might have spared herself becoming one of those very casualties.

Silas, on the other hand, had a genteel side. Even though she had just met him, when she was with him she felt different. She sought for a word to describe it but came up blank. The closest she came was "equal." Blaine kept her on edge, worried that he might find something to disapprove of in her style, her manner, her words. She didn't feel that way with Silas.

He was—a friend. That was it. And it was wonderful. She needed friends.

He and Reverend Tupper called to her. It was time to bundle up again and go to the Robbins's home.

Her scarf fell off, and as she replaced it over her head, she thought of what her hair must look like—probably more was out of the bun than in it at this point. She should just give up and let it go wherever it wanted. It would anyway.

They left the church, and Eliza followed the two men. The weather wasn't improving, she thought as they struggled through the pillow drifts that crisscrossed the road, little fingers of snow that would, with any encouragement from the elements, soon become full-blown snowdrifts. But she'd said she'd help, and she wouldn't go back on her word.

Soon they slowed in front of the white house Paul had pointed out. "It's seen better days," Silas said charitably.

In fact, the steps were slanted, one shutter swung free, and the paint was peeling badly. "Those we'll take care of when spring comes," Reverend Tupper said. "Let's go inside and see what we can do today."

The inside of the house was in better shape. Paul ran to meet them and take their coats, and she heard Edward say to him, "Say, I hear that you were quite observant at the house yesterday. Good job, Paul. I'm proud of you."

Once the coats were off and hung on the coat rack, the children clustered around Silas and peered into the basket containing the turkey dinner, their shouts of glee almost drowning out Jack Robbins's greeting.

"Children," he said, clapping his hands and getting his offspring's attention, "I think we should all introduce ourselves to Miss Davis. I'll start. Miss Davis, I'm Jack Robbins. I think we knew each other a long time ago. It's good to have you back in Remembrance."

The children immediately formed a line, and the oldest boy stepped forward. "I'm Luke. I'm ten."

"You know me. I'm Paul and this is my twin brother Peter, and he's six." The children snickered, and Paul flushed. "We're both six."

"He's silly," said the next to the last child. "I'm Brian, and I'm four, and this is my brother Mark. He's two."

A girl with shy eyes was last. "I'm Analia. I'm five."

"I'm pleased to meet you all," Eliza said, a bit surprised at how much she meant it. She hadn't been around children much, but this group had already shown itself to be special. The few times she had needed to work with children nearby, they hadn't been this well behaved at all.

Within minutes, the turkey was put aside for dinner, safely out of the reach of eager little hands.

"Would you like to meet my wife?" Jack asked.

"Yes, I certainly would," Eliza responded. She tried to tuck her hair back into place, but as usual, it wouldn't stay.

Mary Robbins was a slight thing, very pale and thin, and almost lost in the bedcovers which were tousled and twisted.

She reached a gaunt hand to Eliza. "I'm glad to meet you," she said, her voice as soft and faint as a whisper. "I understand you're a dressmaker and that you've come to help my children not look so much like ragamuffins." She coughed and sank back onto the pillow as if the short conversation exhausted her.

"It's my pleasure. I enjoy sewing. There's something relaxing about it."

Mary's hands plucked uselessly at a blanket that had slipped down. "Would you like me to fix your bedding?" Eliza asked.

The ill woman nodded. "Please."

Eliza straightened the blankets and fluffed the pillows. "There. Now I'd better see what's awaiting me in the mending basket. It's been a delight to meet you."

Mary smiled. "God bless you, Miss Davis."

Eliza touched the woman's hand. "Please, call me Eliza, and I am already blessed."

Reverend Tupper and Jack came into the room, and Eliza left to begin on the sewing.

She and Silas soon settled themselves by the fire. Eliza had a basket of shirts that needed to be mended or cut down, and she studied them carefully, evaluating each one.

He was repairing some of the boys' boots. "I've never done this before, but it's not horribly difficult," he told her as he squinted at the instep of one. "With six children, and five of them boys, I guess boots need to have a longer life than usual."

"Strikes me that it's a lot like basic sewing, isn't it?" She flexed her fingers. The cold had made them clumsy at first, but as they warmed up, the feeling had returned. She turned the red plaid shirt to see if there was any way to salvage it for one more wearer.

"If there's more to it than that, I'm lost," he admitted. "But so far it's been a simple matter of thick thread, a stout needle, and a load of patience."

"That's why I sew." She took up her shears and cut the shirt smaller. "This'll have to be redone. It's torn along the seams. I think this may be the last go-round for this shirt. It's so thin that it's almost transparent. But yes, I do like to sew because I'm so impatient."

He laid the shoe down and stared at her, the flames of the fire reflecting in his pale brown eyes. "That seems odd. Wouldn't it be the other way around? I'd think you'd have to be a patient person to sew."

Eliza laughed. "I wish it were so! I'm very impatient with many things, but sewing makes me slow down, and it gives me time to think."

"What do you think about?"

"Of course I think about the project. I love to watch the flat material become a dress or a shirt or a pair of trousers.

There's such a sense of success about it when it's going well. And when it isn't going well, of course I get frustrated, but I view it like a puzzle, and I can almost always resolve it. I also pray a lot when I sew."

"Really?" He cut the thread he was using and tested the seam. "Good. It'll hold."

"On the long stretches, where I'm finishing a seam or hemming a skirt, I talk to God a lot. The even stitching is the perfect backdrop for prayer. Don't you pray while you work? Or maybe that's not a good idea. You might fall off a ladder."

"And break my precious limb," he finished for her. They both laughed. "I usually pray in the morning and at night before I go to bed, and I say grace before I eat, of course. I also pray during the course of the day, mainly when I have a challenge or I want to take up a cause with God. I must sound like God's neediest child sometimes!"

She spread the pieces of the now cut-up shirt out on the table in front of her. "I'll be praying that this comes together all right. Well, with five boys in the family, it ought to fit one of them."

Jack called them in to eat. The turkey that Mrs. Adams had sent over was carved, and a bowl of potatoes and gravy was placed next to a platter of corn.

The children rushed in, each taking what was clearly their designated spot at the table, from the oldest to the youngest.

"Please, have a seat," Jack said. "I've got two extra chairs here."

"What about Mary? And Reverend Tupper?" Eliza asked.

Jack's face softened. "I always feed Mary first. She ate fairly well today, thanks to this delicious food. The Reverend has gone on to his home, so it's just us."

Silas pulled out a chair for her, and then sat on her left.

Analia was on her right.

"Time for grace," Paul said. "Hold Mr. Collier's hand, Miss Davis. That's how we pray, holding hands."

Peter snickered.

"Not like that, silly," interjected Brian. "They're praying hands, not I-love-you hands."

Silas coughed, and Eliza looked down to hide her smile. She took Analia's hand first and then reached for Silas's. Analia's were warm and sticky, and Silas's were dry and firm.

"Children, hush," Jack said. "Silas, would you say our blessing?"

"Dearest Lord, we thank You for Your gifts, for food, for friendship, for eternal life. May we always keep you close. Amen."

"That was sure short," Paul said. "Reverend Tupper goes on so long the meat gets cold."

The other children shushed him, and the dishes were passed from one to another.

The dinner was excellent and the children well behaved, but Eliza was aware of Silas next to her throughout the meal. *Not I-love-you hands, indeed!*

They spent the rest of the day working together quietly, until at last they decided to quit. Reverend Tupper had already gone back to the church, so they walked together back to the boardinghouse. The sun had set, and the wind had died down. The snow had ended, but a light crystalline shimmer made the air sparkle in the moonlight.

Fairy dust, her mother had called it, and it did look as magical as that. This was the backdrop of beautiful dreams, in which anything could happen.

"I love this," she said, sweeping her hand in front of her. "I'm sure there's some scientific name for the phenomenon—"

He began to interrupt, but she put a gloved hand over his lips. "I don't want to know. It's so beautiful, these tiny speckles of ice floating in the air."

They walked in silence to the boardinghouse, watching the interplay of the crystals and the moonlight. At last, as they reached the door, Eliza paused, reluctant to let the magic end.

"Eliza—" Silas began, but whatever he was about to say was lost as the door flew open and Hyacinth and Edward burst out.

"We're getting married!" Hyacinth sang. "We've decided that we like each other as much in person as we did in letters, so we're going to get married as soon as Edward heals."

"I want to be able to carry my bride across the threshold," Uncle Edward said. "That's the only reason I'd delay matrimony with my Winter Butterfly."

Winter Butterfly? Eliza let it go and hugged her new friend. "That's wonderful!" she said. "Isn't it, Silas?"

He hadn't moved until she spoke. Then he shook his uncle's hand. "Absolutely grand. Absolutely grand."

That moment of hesitation spoke volumes, and Eliza noticed the fleeting disappointment on Hyacinth's and Edward's faces. His approval mattered so much to them.

She diverted them with questions about the upcoming nuptials. Had they spoken to Reverend Tupper? What about a reception afterward? A wedding dress?

"I want you to make the dress," Hyacinth said, her eyes again bright with excitement. "I know just what I want, too. Yellow silk—"

"Yellow silk?" Eliza's thoughts flew to the impracticality of yellow silk in the midst of winter. "Are you sure? Perhaps a soft woolen or even satin, although even one snowflake could spot it forever, would be better."

"She wants yellow silk? Yellow silk she shall have!" Uncle Edward boomed.

Silas stood aside as the wedding plans were quickly spun into place. His lips tightly compressed, his dissatisfaction was evident.

At last he spoke. "I am going home now. Uncle, are you coming with me?"

Uncle Edward turned toward Hyacinth. "The hour is late, dearest. I shall see you on the morrow."

Silas rolled his eyes. "When did you turn into Shakespeare? Honestly!"

"That's not Shakespeare," his uncle responded. "As much as you read, you should know that."

The two quibbled the entire way out of the boardinghouse, and their words carried across the open air as they headed to their house.

"I can't help but feel I'm at the center of some discord between Edward and Silas," Hyacinth said as she shut the front door of the boardinghouse. "Silas doesn't seem to be happy about my marrying his uncle."

Mrs. Adams came into the room and moved around the edges, straightening an antimacassar, adjusting a doily, wiping imaginary dust from a small round table. "Oh, don't mind me," she said. "I'm just tidying up."

A nod of Hyacinth's head indicated that they should go upstairs where they could talk in private, and Eliza followed her into the older woman's room, where Hyacinth sank onto the bed with an exasperated sigh.

"What do you think, Eliza? Silas doesn't seem to be as, well, enthusiastic as I'd hoped he would be."

Eliza detested being caught in the middle, and yet she saw no way to avoid it here unless she spoke carefully. Quickly she prayed for God to guide her words. "I don't know that he has anything against you, Hyacinth. Of course he is concerned. You have to admit that you and Edward met in an unconventional way. You can't blame him for being cautious. He loves his uncle, and he wants to make sure he's doing the right thing."

Hyacinth flung herself back, her arms outstretched. "I *am* the right thing! Why can't he see that?"

"Well," Eliza began, feeling for all the world like she was picking her way through a field of thistles, "I suspect he doesn't know you yet. And he may be concerned that his uncle doesn't know you well enough. Yet."

"But he does. There's nothing hidden in my past. I've led my life as a good Christian woman. I tell you, Eliza, he could hire a detective and I'd come up as clean as new linen. How many women could say that?"

Eliza flinched. It seemed like Blaine Loring had reached into her and seized her heart with his sin-stained fingers. She felt as if she'd never be clean again. The only relief she had was that she hadn't let his advances progress. She had always stopped him. No, the spot on her soul was what she had done to others, on his cue.

Hyacinth switched to the happier topic of her wedding plans, and Eliza let her mind continue to revisit the specter of Blaine Loring. How could she have let herself believe his lies?

Was it wrong to trust so completely? The Bible did caution about this. Matthew 10:16 came easily to her mind: *Behold, I send you forth as sheep in the midst of wolves: be ye therefore wise as serpents, and harmless as doves.*

"You're not listening," Hyacinth said accusingly, with a playful glint in her eyes, her earlier distress clearly laid aside.

"I must be tired," Eliza said. It was true. She was. It had been a long day with many unexpected twists and turns.

Back in her room, she got ready for bed quickly. Once she'd buried herself under the quilt and the extra blanket from the chest at the bottom of the mattress—the night was indeed cold—she closed her eyes and thought again about the verse.

Sheep. Wolves. Serpents. Doves. It was quite a menagerie for so few words but its meaning was clear. If only she'd heeded it earlier.

She said her prayers and turned over, ready to sleep, when one final thought crossed her mind. *Harmless as doves.* It was beautiful. She could do that. She could be as harmless as a dove.

※

Silas helped his uncle to his bedroom, noting that each evening the trip seemed to get easier. His ankle was healing.

"I'd like to talk to you before we turn in, Silas," Uncle Edward said as he hobbled into his room. "Have a seat."

Silas sank into the chair beside the small table in his uncle's room. Fortunately it wasn't one that Uncle Edward had recovered in his remodeling frenzy, so he was in no imminent danger of sliding off.

His uncle patted Silas's shoulder, and for the first time, Silas noticed how rheumatism had swollen the joints. Carpentry must be painful for him.

"Silas, don't be too harsh with Hyacinth and me. I do love her."

"Of course you do."

Edward sighed. "I do. I don't expect you to understand, Silas, at least not in your brain. Please try to understand in your heart. I never married, you know that. I told myself that was fine, and I guess it was. I had the carpentry business, but after a while, it all wears thin. I don't know how to explain it."

"You don't need to." The last thing he wanted was to hear his uncle wax rhapsodic about his Chicago sweetheart.

"I do need to. You've been like a son to me. But I'd like a wife. I want to be loved, to be held in a woman's embrace. I want to wake up to the smell of lilacs on my pillow. I want—"

The smell of lilacs. Or soap, like Eliza. In a town that often didn't smell very good at all, a woman's scent had great power.

He was getting as fanciful as his uncle.

He could understand the need to be loved, but what if Hyacinth wasn't the right one? His uncle had spent his entire life single. Was he leaping headfirst into trouble by choosing the first woman he courted?

It all seemed so impetuous. And impetuous meant silly.

"Good night." Silas left his uncle's bedroom, shutting the door and heading to his own room.

What a day! He had worried about his own future, what he would do if Hyacinth came into the household, and now, all of his concerns about that disappeared. Like early snowflakes that evaporated before landing on the ground, the burden he'd carried about his livelihood vanished.

He would have the carpentry business. His financial future was settled. The irony of it struck him—if Hyacinth hadn't come into his uncle's life, this security might have remained elusive.

Nothing was going to ever be the same in his life again, and he had to admit that some of that came from a woman named Eliza.

She fit in so easily at church and with the Robbins family. Eliza had a rare talent for gentleness and yet he also saw a great source of strength. He had never met anyone quite like her.

Eager to get his mind off the strange turn of events, he opened *Professor Barkley's Patented Five Year Plan for Success*.

He was supposed to be reading these in the morning, not the evening, and he felt a twinge of guilt about that. Tomorrow he'd change.

The day's study was about trust. Professor Barkley pointed out that one must trust in the Lord's guidance rather than the often-faulty perceptions of man. He cited some direct advice from the Bible, which was the verse for the day. It was Proverbs 3:5–6: *Trust in the LORD with all thine heart; and lean not unto thine own understanding. In all thy ways acknowledge him, and he shall direct thy paths.*

Silas shut the book. It was excellent advice but, like much excellent advice, hard to put into action.

He wondered how Eliza fit into God's ways for him. The thought carried him into sleep, and sleep carried him into dreams, dreams sprinkled with a magical glimmer.

five

Time was flying by. Eliza counted the days she'd been in Remembrance—almost three weeks now. She'd been so busy at the Robbins's house that she'd barely had time to think.

Hyacinth handed the platter of hotcakes to Eliza. "I could eat all of these, they're so good, but I'd be waddling down the aisle if I do. You'd better take them."

"If one of us has to be waddling around, it might as well be me." Eliza took another hotcake. They *were* good.

"Tell me about yesterday. How was it?" Hyacinth took a sip of her tea as she waited for Eliza's answer.

"The family certainly does need help. The mother is so sick, and the father is stretched as far as he can go, I'm afraid. I spent all of my time there trying to do something with the children's clothing. They have six children, and five of them are boys."

"How sad. Were you able to mend the clothing?"

Sudden tears crowded behind Eliza's eyes, and she made a great point of buttering the hotcakes. Finally she said, "I did what I could. The youngest one, poor thing, is getting the worst of it. By the time the clothing gets to him, the material in the shirts and trousers is worn almost through. It seems like as soon as I mend something, it comes back to me with more repair needed. The fabric is simply giving out."

"Can we get some more yardage from the mercantile?" Hyacinth asked. "I'd like to help in some way, but I'm not a seamstress and I'm not a carpenter, and it's been a long time since I've been around children, but I could buy several yards if that would help."

"It would! Hyacinth, you're a blessing for all of us."

Her offer was the answer to a prayer. Eliza had spent several days at the Robbins's house, dissecting shirt after shirt to make them last for one more wearer, one more season. Just the day before, as she stitched a side seam, the back split open, it was so worn. Her sewing was slow. Not only was she hampered by the lack of her sewing machine, she was frustrated by the condition of the fabric. Some of it was so thin that it almost came apart in her hands.

"Let's go over as soon as the store opens, then, and we can select some new fabric," Hyacinth said, her face glowing as she planned the trip. "And let's make sure the littlest boy gets a new shirt. Actually, let's see if we can't find enough for everyone to have something new."

"It'll mean so much to them." The family had done with so little for so long that the new clothing—from new fabric— would be a real treat for them.

The woman truly had a heart of gold, Eliza thought. She'd make sure that Silas knew about Hyacinth's offer. Maybe that would help him see her in a better light.

"As much as I like Mrs. Adams, and I do like her and she certainly can cook circles around me," Hyacinth said as they left the boardinghouse, "I'm not complaining, mind you, or maybe I am, but I'm feeling a bit stifled with Mrs. Adams always looking over my shoulder. I'm used to living on my own, having no one to answer to but myself and God.

"Well, I'm not in the house yet, am I? We're stuck forever in the boardinghouse. We'll grow old together there, you and I. But we'll have our breakfast at seven, our dinner at noon, and our supper at six. And between three and five on

Saturdays and Sundays, we can receive gentlemen callers in the parlor. Oh, we have a grand life ahead of us, Eliza."

They stopped and peeked in the window at the small house. "I think I'm going to have a talk with Edward about this," Hyacinth declared. "It doesn't look as if a single thing has been done to it."

Eliza stood on her tiptoes and stared through the grimy panes. "It does need a good cleaning."

Hyacinth shook her head and sighed. "Something has to be done."

After one last look through the window, they left the house and headed for the store.

Walking into the mercantile was like stepping into a kaleidoscope. Dazzling in the early morning sunlight, colors were jumbled together. Green pickles in brown barrels and red licorice in rainbowed glass. Silvery nails and bronze tacks. Pink combs and yellow brushes. In the sewing section, spools of ribbons slid on a rod, spilling out in a rainbow of bright stripes; bolts of calico leaned against workaday chambray and broadcloth; thread glowed in multi-hued splendor.

"I suppose this is nothing like you're used to," Hyacinth whispered as they approached the fabric. "The shops in St. Paul must be fantastic."

Eliza pulled a strand of chocolate brown ribbon between her fingers. Its velvety texture would make a striking detail on a winter dress. "I generally didn't have the option of selecting the material. I did to-order dressmaking."

"Look at this pattern, these tiny blue flowers against the cream. Wouldn't it be the perfect material for a young girl's dress?"

It would look striking with Analia's chestnut hair. Eliza thought of the girl with the sad eyes, and an idea came to her. Analia was so quiet that it was easy to forget her as she curled in the corner with her books and dolls, especially with five boisterous brothers demanding attention.

Eliza looked at Hyacinth, now leafing through a copy of *Godey's* that she suspected was quite out-of-date, and had an idea.

"I'll be going over to the Robbins home again later today. Why don't you come with me? I'll need to take more measurements and do a bit of fitting work, and I can always use some help."

Hyacinth put down the magazine. "I don't know a thing about it, but that's never stopped me before," she declared.

Eliza smiled. Hyacinth's ready good humor was going to be a blessing to her as she remade her life in Remembrance.

They selected utilitarian thick cotton to make trousers for the boys, bright plaids for shirts to replace the faded and worn ones Eliza had been trying to repair, and the blue and cream floral as well as a soft pink and white striped fabric for dresses for Analia. At the last minute, Hyacinth added a delicate spring green flannel for a nightgown for Mary.

"Do you want a peppermint stick?" Hyacinth asked as they approached the cash register. "I confess I have a weakness for them." She picked one out of the glass jar on the counter. "One for you, too?"

"Of course! Peppermint and snow. They go together, don't they?"

At last they left the store, their bulky packages balanced carefully, and they picked their way across the snowy road to the Robbins's house. "We should have gotten Silas to help us," Hyacinth panted as one of the bundles nearly slipped out of her grasp.

"He's already there. They started early because they're

working in the pantry area today, putting up new shelves, and want to get them done by the end of the week." She tucked her chin deeper into her scarf.

"Will it take that long? I'd think they could do that in a day or two."

Eliza laughed. "Not with five boys eager to 'help.' That makes every project last even longer."

"I suppose it would. My son Thomas nearly drove his father to the madhouse, dogging his every footstep. He wanted to know what every seed was that his father planted, how long it took to come through the earth, how seeds ate—"

"How seeds ate? What kind of question is that?"

"A Thomas question. He was full of them. How do seeds eat? Do caterpillars dream while they're in the cocoon, and do they dream caterpillar dreams or butterfly dreams? He teaches at a college in New York now."

"You must be very proud of him."

"I am. Oh, I am."

"This is the house, by the way," Eliza said.

"I'm so glad. My fingers are frozen into immovable sticks. I'm going to have to knit some warmer mittens, and soon!"

They were met at the door by all of the children. "What did you bring?" they chimed.

"Nothing more exciting than fabric, I'm sorry to say," Eliza said. "Let's go to the table and open these packages and you can take a look at what your new clothes will be made out of."

The children danced happily to the table and began opening the packages. Brian, the four-year-old, whooped. "Are these for us? There are—let me count. One, two, three, four, five, six, seven, eight, nine, ten, eleven! Eleven peppermint sticks."

"Silly." Luke, his older brother, took the candies away from him and put them back inside the wrapping. "That doesn't even make sense. There are six of us children, and Mother and Father. That's eight."

Hyacinth laughed. "And Mr. Collier and Miss Davis and myself. That makes eleven. Here, my darlings, one for each of you, one for your father, one for your mother, and please take one to Mr. Collier, also. But don't spoil your dinner!" Hyacinth's last words were lost to the shouts of joy from the children as they each took a peppermint stick and then argued over who would take the others to the adults. The littlest ones were victorious, and soon all of them, adults and children alike, held a candy stick.

Silas popped out from the pantry area. His hair was liberally dusted with sawdust, and his face had a big smear of something dark on it. A peppermint stick stuck out of his mouth like a striped cigar. "What a treat!" he exclaimed. "Thank you so much! I haven't had one of these in years."

"Hyacinth got them," Eliza said. "The *children* are certainly enjoying theirs." She couldn't resist just a bit of teasing.

"You don't have one?" he countered, coming close enough that she could smell the clean aroma of newly sawed wood mingled with the crisp scent of peppermint. A few shavings fell from his arm as he pointed to her hand, which held her own peppermint stick. "Let me guess. You're a savorer, someone who makes the candy last as long as possible. This peppermint stick will probably last you a week."

She could feel the flush that crept up her neck. "Well, yes. That way I can enjoy it longer."

"But this way—" He took a bite from his with a great crunch. "This way, you get the full effects of the mint. And you get to chew it. That, my dear girl, is the way to eat a peppermint stick."

Eliza cleared her throat. "I shall certainly keep that in mind." Gratefully she seized on the conversation happening behind her.

Hyacinth and Analia were examining the opened packets from the store. Analia's small fingers caressed the striped fabric. "Do you like it?" Hyacinth asked quietly. "It's going to look so pretty with your dark hair and eyes."

"It looks like my peppermint stick."

"Oh, it does! It's pink and white, isn't it?" Hyacinth looked at Eliza and winked. "Let's ask Miss Davis if she might do this first then."

Analia shook her head. "No."

Eliza knelt down. "No? Analia, why not? You'll look like a princess in it."

"Make my mother's gown first. Please."

Everything seemed to slow. Even the clock's ticking lagged. Eliza blinked back the tears that stung her eyes. She wrapped Analia in her arms and held her closely against her. "Honey, I will. Your mother's first, and then yours. You are such a sweet, thoughtful girl."

Something in her heart moved as if a piece that had been broken slid back into place.

"Why don't you come with me?" Hyacinth said, holding out her hand to Analia at last. "Let's braid your hair, and then why don't you and I go in and visit with your mother for a while? We'll have some lady talk."

Eliza worked near the window, cutting and pinning the pale green fabric for Mary Robbins's nightgown. She wished she'd been able to bring her sewing machine with her from St. Paul, but it was at the shop, and she had left it behind. Sewing went so much faster with the machine. She'd be able to have all the clothing made in a third of the time it would take her to hand-stitch it.

As it was, all this sewing was going to take at least a month and a half. With a sewing machine, she could probably get it done in two weeks. Then she'd feel better taking some extra care with the hand finishing, making sure everything was exactly right.

Still, speed came with a price. Here, she'd be around Silas. And, she had to admit as she bent over the green cloth, she was enjoying it. There was something about that solemn expression that could suddenly open with a smile that she looked forward to seeing every day.

Remembrance was fitting her quite well. She might just stay.

&

"Yes, I went over there," Silas said to his uncle for what seemed like the twentieth time in the last half hour. "Yes. I gave them the message. Yes, they said they'd come."

Uncle Edward struggled to his feet and limped over to the window. "You're sure?"

"Yes! And use your cane, please! I don't want you falling and breaking your other precious limb."

"My *what*?" his uncle boomed.

"Oh, never mind." Silas knew he was snappish but was just cranky enough not to care. God must be challenging him all the time, he thought, to be more accepting of change because He certainly provided enough learning experiences.

Even Professor Barkley seemed in on it. The day's lesson was titled, "How to Take Control of the Future." They'd already covered that earlier, with the "Expect the Unexpected" lesson. Today Professor Barkley advised that although one cannot control the future—it is, after all, written by God's hand—one can prepare for what lies ahead.

He mulled it over, just as he had the earlier lesson. Professor

Barkley clearly didn't consider them to be the same subjects, so what was Silas missing? Maybe if one could expect what they weren't expecting, they could control what they couldn't control?

It made his head hurt.

Everything in his life was beyond his control.

From the time he chose to come to live with his uncle as a young lad, he had been like a leaf in a stream, sent whichever way the current sent him. He had two choices: printing or carpentry.

The oddest part was that he found he possessed a true talent for carpentry. It was, as Uncle Edward was wont to remind him, a sacred profession, too, for the blessed Jesus had Himself been a carpenter.

Then his uncle had delivered the biggest surprise: He was hoping to marry someone he'd never met, never even seen.

The surprises just kept on. The broken ankle. The arrival of Hyacinth—and Eliza.Oh, Professor Barkley had let him down this time. Even he couldn't have been prepared for any of this.

"I see them!" Uncle Edward crowed, and he hobbled happily to the front door.

Eliza and Hyacinth entered the house with a covered basket that emitted the heavenly aroma of cinnamon and brown sugar. Uncle Edward investigated the contents greedily. "Good! Cookies! I've got just the platter for them—" His sentence trailed off as he and Hyacinth left the room.

"Did you make them?" Silas asked Eliza.

"Do you really think that Mrs. Adams would let me in her kitchen?" Eliza began to unwind her scarf. "Ha!"

He helped her out of her coat, breathing in her clean scent and trying to ignore the little curl that had escaped the thick bun and spiraled down her neck behind her ear, the wayward coil as brown as the cinnamon-dusted cookies she carried in.

She turned back to him, automatically touching her hair to straighten it, and he almost sighed aloud when her fingers found the lock and pressed it back into the bun. "Honestly, sometimes I think you men are the lucky ones with the short hair. There are days when I would love to just chop this all off!"

Before he could respond, Hyacinth rejoined them, carrying a tray with cups of tea and the cookies. "We'll have them in here," Uncle Edward said, who was right behind her, "and take advantage of the fireplace and the sunshine."

Silas removed the newspaper from the seat beside him and tossed it onto the small reading table. Eliza immediately picked it up. "I haven't seen a newspaper since I came here!" she said. "Oh, it's from Duluth."

"My darling Hyacinth and I are dreaming of making our nest there," Uncle Edward said, beaming at his bride-to-be. "We'll live in our cottage by the sea—"

"Lake Superior is not a sea," Silas interjected, not liking his petulant tone but unable to stop himself. "It's a Great Lake. There are five of them. Lake Superior. Lake Huron. Lake Michigan. Lake Ontario. Lake Erie."

"Then we'll live in our cottage by the Great Lake," Uncle Edward said, obviously annoyed with his nephew. "Happy?"

"I'm just pointing out to you that Duluth isn't on a sea. That's all. It's on Lake Superior." Silas scowled.

"Wait!" Eliza waved her hands in front of her. "Stop! I don't care if Duluth is on the edge of the Arctic Ocean or the Nile River. What does it matter?"

"Indeed." Uncle Edward picked up the newspaper. "I've been having this sent to me. It's a dandy paper, too. Not only does it keep me up on what's happening there, it's got news from the rest of the state. Here's a bit about the St. Paul Ice Carnival. Now there's some spectacular thinking going on in the capital."

Hyacinth read over his shoulder. "What an interesting idea! There are all sorts of things planned, even a palace made entirely of ice! Eliza, have you heard of this?"

Eliza nodded. "The minister of the church I went to in St. Paul, Reverend Everett, told me about it. They're quite excited about it. His daughter, Christal, was a friend of mine, and she was very interested in it. I'll have to have her tell me all about it, the next time I see her."

"And here's another story of interest," Edward said, reading further. "Down in Mankato, along the Minnesota River, they're building a new courthouse."

Silas yawned. "All very interesting, Uncle."

"Not wild enough for you?" his uncle asked with a sharp glare at Silas. "Then maybe you'll like this story. Some sly trickster in St. Paul has been discovered taking advantage of the maidenly workforce there. Apparently he coaxes them into believing he's in love with them by filling their minds with pledges of a secure monetary future while—"

Eliza gasped, and her hand moved quickly to her throat. "No!"

Silas leaped up and went to her, kneeling in front of her. "Eliza, are you feeling unwell?"

All the color drained from her face, and her breathing was shallow. He put his fingers over her wrist and frowned.

"Your pulse is racing. Eliza! Are you all right?" he asked again, this time a bit louder.

"I'm fine," she said, fluttering her hand in front of her face. "I feel like such a goose for alarming you. I couldn't help but think that I used to live in St. Paul, and it was probably only

His mercies that I escaped this beast. What was his name again, Edward?"

"Let me see." Uncle Edward scanned the article. "Oh, yes, here it is. The scoundrel's name is Loring. Blaine Loring."

six

Eliza forced herself to breathe normally. She was here, safe, in Remembrance. There was nothing to tie her to this monster anymore. She thought he was merely a two-timing Lothario—and that had cut deeply, right into her heart—and now she was learning he was also a criminal. She was lucky to have gotten away from him before he dragged her into his sordid activities.

Her mind busily tried to sort the new information out, even as those around her continued to speak, their voices muted as the pounding in her head grew. What she had done—that was legitimate. It had to be.

"The story becomes more interesting," Uncle Edward said. "Listen to this: 'Loring is assumed to have taken financial as well as romantic liberties with the young women by conniving them into investing in a complicated scheme in which only he benefits. Apparently the young women, who are maids and seamstresses and nannies, were encouraged by Loring's empty words to take part in his malevolent plan, turning their savings over to him. How Loring was able to exact the exchange of money for promises, and at such magnitude, has not been discovered, but an investigation is underway, and authorities have vowed that all parties will be prosecuted to the full extent of the law.'"

"Oh, Eliza, I am so glad you didn't get mixed up with this nasty fellow," Hyacinth said as she stirred sugar into her tea. "He sounds like just the kind of person who could easily ruin your life."

Eliza's heart pounded so loudly she thought that certainly they all could hear it. The kind of person who could easily ruin her life? Indeed.

"Not our Eliza!" Uncle Edward scoffed. "Why, she's too intelligent to get sucked into one of those setups. And that's just what it is. A setup. Some man with absolutely no moral backbone wastes all of the brains God gave him by trying to figure how to get rich without putting forth any effort, when in reality, it's probably more work that way than it would be if he'd just gone out and gotten a job, like the rest of the world."

"Now, dearest Edward, calm down. That Loring man is an animal, and I'm glad that his fiendish design is coming down around his head. Have another cookie."

Have another cookie. If only it could be that easy. Eliza wanted to put her hands over her ears and stop the rushing sound that kept echoing in her head.

This was far worse than finding the man she loved in the arms of another woman. Far worse than finding out that he hadn't cared at all for her.

How could she not have seen it? She let herself get so caught up in his web of false flattery that she hadn't seen the truth, even when it was right in front of her.

She was a lowly seamstress; he was a wealthy investor. She had been so blinded by his attention to her that she'd never wondered what such an apparently rich and influential man would see in her.

All the signs were there from the beginning.

He sought her out. His gifts were not from his heart but from his plan—to get her so overcome with the glitter that she wouldn't see the tarnish.

She'd walked right into his treachery. He had an investment opportunity, he told her, that he wanted to open to the young women in service to the wealthy. It was a way for them to improve their lots in life—the same way, he so winningly pointed out—that the rich got richer, through investment.

He'd sounded as if he thought only of these poor girls, and his false altruism made him even more appealing to her.

So she very helpfully went out and encouraged these same women to give him their money.

How could she have been so stupid?

She had been his accomplice in this horrible plot. Now she knew why he had been so interested in her. She'd been so blind, so willing to believe his oily lies that she fell right into his trap.

"We're so lucky to be in Remembrance, away from people like that," Hyacinth said, shuddering. "Can you imagine how those poor women feel?"

Edward nodded. "There are some men who feel that innocence is a challenge."

"Absolutely," Hyacinth agreed, "and too often we assume that innocence is a physical matter, when in fact true innocence lives in the soul, far beyond the reach of such men."

Silas dismissed the entire conversation. "Certainly we can discuss something other than this beast in St. Paul. He isn't worthy of our words."

Eliza swallowed hard and stared out the window. Snow had started to fall again, a very pretty snow for the onset of evening. Oversized white fluffs that drifted slowly were silhouetted against the deep twilight-blue sky, undisturbed by even the faintest touch of wind.

The snow would quickly cover the disturbed and uneven patches where boys had had snowball fights, or the mud-colored ruts in the road that would be re-formed into treacherous muck in the spring melt. All they'd see tomorrow would be smooth unbroken snow, clean and fresh.

"Eliza?"

She realized that the others were watching her expectantly, waiting for an answer to a question she hadn't heard. "I'm sorry. I'm afraid you've caught me daydreaming." She managed a light laugh that didn't sound to her as if it would fool anyone.

"I mentioned the house by the mercantile," Hyacinth said, "and I said we'd stopped by and nothing seemed to have been touched in it."

"It seemed quite abandoned." Eliza seized on the chance to discuss a different subject. "The only footsteps in the snow were ours, so clearly no one else had been by recently."

Edward buried his face in the newspaper again. "Here's more news of interest. Apparently the precipitation in Duluth last month—"

Silas, Eliza realized, was no longer slouched in the chair. He was sitting up, staring at his uncle sharply.

"The house by the mercantile?" Silas repeated. "What house? Not the old Lindstrom house!"

"Well," his uncle replied, only half-lowering the paper, "it's a good sturdy house."

"Would you like to fill me in on this, Uncle?"

"It's a good, solid house."

"So is this one."

"It's an investment."

Eliza trembled at the term. If she never heard of investments again, it would be fine with her.

"Are you telling me," Silas continued in the same low voice, "that you're thinking of buying it?"

The newspaper went back up.

"Uncle Edward, what aren't you telling me?"

The silence from behind the newspaper seemed to grow.

Silas sat back and sighed. "You already bought it. That's just foolish. You bought it just so Hyacinth would have a place to stay?" He paused. "Or for me to stay? Is that it?"

"Not exactly." Edward folded the paper neatly, obviously stalling for time. Then he looked at his nephew. "I've owned it for a while. I keep meaning to get over there and work on it but—" He motioned toward his ankle. "It seems like it's always been one thing or another."

"Why on earth, though?"

"The Lindstroms, you know, left, and their daughter and her husband moved in, but he got that job in Chicago, and they moved, and an older man moved in, but he got so he couldn't walk and his grandchildren came and got him, and then that kind young man stayed until—"

"I know all this. What I don't know is why you now own it."

"Because that young fellow was in love with a woman living in Rochester, and he couldn't bear to be apart from her, and he wanted to go to be with her, and I bought the house so he'd have the money to go up to Rochester and be with her. There. That's it. I'm a romantic old sap."

"I see. Well."

"And it worked out perfectly, because all we have to do is fix it up a bit, and it'll be just right for what we need now."

"What kind of shape is it in?" Silas asked. "Nobody's lived in it since, when, late October? November? It'll need some work."

"I don't rightly know," Edward said. "I meant to go over there but then I got busy and one thing led to another and then next thing I knew I was flying off the ladder and cracking the bone in my ankle here. I guess I got excited about Petunia Blossom coming out to Remembrance and just kind of forgot."

Petunia Blossom. Now there was a new one. Even in her

distress, it made Eliza smile.

"Before you plan further," Silas interjected, "let me go over and take a look at it. The house may not be sound anymore."

"Good idea," Edward said. "You're right. A house is an investment, and we need to keep that in mind. It's quite unfortunate that those poor young women in St. Paul hadn't done that before giving that reprobate their money. If they'd been a bit wiser, they wouldn't be in the situation they are today. Makes me wonder, though, if there wasn't some kind of an insider involved, someone who'd be able to convince these women that their money was safe."

It was too much for her.

"Excuse me," she said, standing rather quickly. "I don't feel at all well, and I think I'd better go back to the boardinghouse. Please excuse me."

She knew that they were staring at her, astonished at the sudden change in her, but she had to leave. She needed to be alone and work this out. She had to talk to God—and to herself.

Buttoning her coat as she closed the door behind her, she was only slightly aware that the soft snow had now turned to sleet. Nothing in the present mattered. Only the past was important today.

She strode, blindly, down the road and across the town square to the boardinghouse.

"Did they like the cookies—" Mrs. Adams began when Eliza pushed the front door open, but she could only duck her head and run up the stairs to her room.

Please, don't let anyone knock on my door and ask if I'm all right, she pleaded with God as she slipped out of her coat and let it fall to the floor. *I can't talk to anyone. I can't. Only You.*

She went to her favorite spot in the room, the window seat,

and put her head on the cool wooden ledge.

Help me, she pleaded. *Dearest God, what should I do?*

The past began to march past her in a lurid parade. Blaine Loring, dressed as he always was, in an impeccable suit with a gold tiepin, courting her with flowers and poetry and trinkets. He loved her so much, he'd told her, that not only would he line her path with rose petals, he'd do the same with her friends.

All they had to do—

She stopped. The memory was like a knife jabbed deeply into her heart, but she forced herself to go on.

All they had to do was give him part of their wages, meager though they might be, and he'd invest them in a no-fail venture that would double, triple, or even quadruple their portions. One day, he told her, her friends could hire their current employers to be *their* maids, *their* seamstresses, *their* nannies.

It was a delicious lure, and she fell for it. For the next eighteen months, she encouraged her friends to turn over as much of their earnings to him as they could. Week after week, month after month, they all scraped yet another layer off their expenses, because they had been assured of a return that would make it all worthwhile.

Apparently this was the biggest of his lies. And worst of all, she'd pledged that his honesty was unquestionable, and because of that—because of *that*—they trusted him with their money.

Her father raised her to be as straight with people as possible. She thought she had been, but she believed the lies, too.

Fool. That's what she was, a fool.

God, please help me. Please. I don't know what to do. Please.

It was the only prayer she could come up with. Visions of the young women who so innocently handed over their savings floated in front of her eyes. Penny by penny, nickel by nickel, she had helped him rob them.

The verse from Matthew floated back into her mind: *Behold, I send you forth as sheep in the midst of wolves: be ye therefore wise as serpents, and harmless as doves.*

There was the warning, right in front of her. Every word, every single word, applied to what happened. Yet still she hadn't seen it, her head had been so completely turned with his fancy words and slick phrases.

She hadn't been harmless. That was what would haunt her.

Would they ever forgive her? Could she ever forgive herself?

Maybe in a legal world, she wasn't guilty of anything except misguided faith. She sat up abruptly. What was it that Edward read from the newspaper? Something about the authorities planning to search for Blaine Loring's accomplices?

She couldn't breathe as she realized what that meant.

The police wanted her, too.

≈

Silas paced in his room. He was done with the unexpected. It never seemed to be good news, and the events of the day proved it once again. He watched Eliza as his uncle read the news aloud, and he'd seen her reaction. Then when Edward brought up the subject again, she grew as pale as the snow-covered lawn and fled from the house. It was clear what had happened.

She'd invested heavily in this crook's scheme and gauging from her reaction, she'd lost quite a lot of money in it. He rubbed his forehead and frowned.

Was there anything he could do to help her? He wasn't a rich man, but he wasn't poor either. Yet somehow, offering her money seemed wrong. Even though his intentions were the best, considering how she'd lost her investment, his move might be misread.

He could wait for her to broach the subject herself. Immediately he rejected that idea. She wasn't the kind to do that. She was undoubtedly embarrassed by what happened.

What *had* happened, anyway? The newspaper provided only the vaguest skeleton of events. He wanted to know how she came to be involved and how deeply she was affected.

He needed to know how much was her money—and how much was her heart.

Silas walked to the window and looked out. He couldn't see the boardinghouse, but he knew where it was—just beyond that set of trees and that cluster of houses, down the road and around the corner.

Tonight it felt as if it were at the end of the universe.

The clock downstairs chimed twice. Two a.m. He'd be a wreck in the morning if he didn't get some sleep.

He climbed into bed and, as always, reviewed Professor Barkley's memory verse for the day. It was Proverbs 25:25: *As cold waters to a thirsty soul, so is good news from a far country.*

There certainly was news from a far country—that is, if one considered Duluth and St. Paul "far countries" rather than "far cities"—but how this could possibly be considered "good news" was beyond him.

He gave up trying to make sense of it and, as he succumbed to sleep, a prayer for Eliza was on his lips. . .and his heart.

seven

The days marched forward relentlessly, with no respite in sight. When Eliza did sleep, it was too lightly to be restorative. She spent most of the nights in a drowsy torpor, too anxious to sleep and too tired to rouse herself.

A tentative knock on the door startled Eliza. She sat up and stretched, every muscle in her back and neck screaming in protest. She must have finally fallen asleep at the window seat, her head cradled on her arm.

This had to end—soon. For almost two weeks the guilt had been building until her stomach throbbed from it, her head shrieked in pain, and her soul was sick. She tried to reason her way out of it, to convince herself that she couldn't be held accountable for something she didn't know about, but it didn't help. All she could think about were the women who gave Blaine Loring their money, simply because they trusted her.

Maybe in a court of law she wouldn't be considered responsible, but she couldn't shake the knowledge of her culpability.

She stood and made her way to the door. Hyacinth stood there, a steaming cup of tea and a plate of toast in her hands. "How are you feeling?"

Hyacinth didn't need to say more. Eliza knew that the older woman's eyes had scanned her room and had seen the bed still not slept in, had taken note of her clothing that she had worn the day before and which was now quite wrinkled.

She'd only gone out when absolutely necessary, pleading a headache the week before when church time came around. It wasn't a lie. Her temples pounded from lack of sleep and worry.

"Are you sick?" Hyacinth persisted gently. "Should I find a doctor?"

Eliza shook her head. "No, no doctor."

"Do you want to talk about it?"

It wasn't an easy question to answer. She did want to, but not yet. Not until she had sorted through everything that was plaguing her.

"Dear, if you do decide you want a sympathetic ear, I've got two. Take it on your own time. Are you hungry? Mrs. Adams sent this up."

The tea and toast smelled heavenly, and she gratefully took them. "I'm sorry," she managed to say, working the words past the dry lump in her throat that wouldn't go away. "It's not that I'm trying to avoid you, or anyone, for that matter. I've got something sitting heavily on my mind."

Hyacinth patted her arm. "You take your time. But if you want to go to church with us, taking your time isn't an option. We're leaving on the dot of eight, you know, which is in twenty minutes."

Time with God in His own house sounded like a wonderful idea. She spoke around the pulsing throb that settled behind her ears. "I'll hurry."

"Good," Hyacinth pronounced. "I'm glad."

As soon as the older woman left, Eliza hurried to get ready for worship. In between bits of toast and sips of tea, she washed her face, rebraided her hair, and changed her dress.

Soon she was walking down the road to the church with Hyacinth and Mrs. Adams. The temperature had risen, and with the sun shining so brightly, she could almost smell spring ahead.

At the front of the church, the weather was the topic of conversation.

"It's the January thaw," one man said. "It happens every year. It's just running late a bit. Doesn't mean a thing. Soon enough the temperature will drop and we'll be shivering again."

"Of course it's the January thaw," another answered, "but it's God's way of saying that the winter will end and that spring will come."

"Science versus poetry," Hyacinth murmured to Eliza. "It's a battle that will never end."

"I hope poetry wins." Being able to walk outside without burying her face in her scarf was liberating. With the sun on her face, she managed to let herself relax and enjoy the brief walk.

Hyacinth led her right to the pew where Silas and Edward were sitting. Both men looked at her with concern but neither said a word. Never before had Eliza appreciated silence so much.

"Today's sermon is about housekeeping," Reverend Tupper began. "Spiritual housekeeping, that is. It comes right from the Fifty-First Psalm: 'Create in me a clean heart, O God.' I'd like us all to think about how clean our hearts are. Do you need to do some spiritual housekeeping?"

Eliza leaned forward. The words were startlingly apropos, and she clung onto every one.

"The psalmist seems to be telling us that God can do it for us," the minister continued. "Is he saying that God is like a hired man, maybe a butler sweeping the crumbs away from our banquet of a sinful life? 'Create in me a clean heart, O God.' What do those words mean? We tell God what to do, and He does it? We want him to take away our sins, and He does it? Is this verse a command to God?"

The answer came to her so clearly that she thought she must have spoken it aloud. It wasn't a command; it was a plea. She wanted a clean heart. Desperately.

Reverend Tupper continued. "This is a very personal verse. I imagine that every one of you is sitting in your pew, interpreting the words' meaning as they apply to your own life's needs, and for each of us, that meaning will be different. These words strike right to the need of the human existence."

Behind her, a sleeping child awoke and was promptly quieted by its mother. Other than that, the church was silent as the congregation listened intently.

" 'Create in me a clean heart.' The words sum up the earthly situation and the basic quest of the Christian. We're all looking to make our hearts clean. But how? Is it God's responsibility? Let's read further."

He opened his worn Bible and read the entire psalm aloud. "Notice that the psalmist asks God to wash him, to purge him. He asks God not to put him aside, and not to hold back His love. 'Restore unto me the joy of thy salvation,' he begs. He needs God. He knows God, but something has come between him and the Lord. He's penitent, and he wants to make it right."

The minister closed the Bible. "This psalm addresses the importance of coming before God Himself, and asking His help. Isn't that," Reverend Tupper said softly, "what we need to do? All of us? He knows it. We just have to ask."

She did want a clean heart. She knew that only God could make it happen—but she had to be repentant. She had to ask for it. She had to want it with all her being. It wasn't just going to happen.

But what was she supposed to do? What did God want her to do? How, exactly, was she to do her own spiritual housecleaning?

The sermon was over, and the congregation stood to sing the final hymn. She sang the words but her mind was still on the sermon. The hymn ended, the blessing was given, and she didn't move, too absorbed in her self-questioning.

Hyacinth nudged her. "I think the service is over."

Eliza came back to earth with a start. "Of course. I'm sorry. I was completely lost in thought."

"That's the way a good sermon should end," Edward declared stoutly. "It's like a solid meal for the soul that lasts all week long."

"I like that." Eliza turned to Silas. "Your uncle has a way with words, doesn't he?"

Silas made a sound like a cross between a snort and a sniff. "He's quite the Nathaniel Hawthorne, that one."

If she hadn't been in church, she might have argued his attitude, but the aura of thoughtful worship held her tightly, and she was not going to let it go. Instead, she paused to let an elderly woman step in front of her, taking advantage of the break to focus away from Silas's sneering words.

"Sorry."

The word was muttered so low, that for a moment she wasn't sure if she'd imagined it. A quick glance over her shoulder showed that Silas had, in fact, spoken.

"It's just that—" he began, but he let his voice trail off and he shook his head. "Sorry," he repeated as the cluster of worshipers in the aisle began to move again.

She might have pursued it further had not she heard her name called.

"Miss Davis! Mrs. Mason!" Mrs. Adams bustled through the congregation still waiting to leave the sanctuary.

Eliza stopped, but Hyacinth had already moved out of the church ahead of her with Edward.

"Miss Davis, I would like to discuss something with you and Mrs. Mason. You are coming back for dinner, are you not? You're not going to the Collier house."

Eliza noticed it wasn't a question, but rather a statement. "I hadn't—" she began, and Mrs. Adams nodded.

"I'd like to meet with you after dinner today." She buttoned her coat to the top, wrapped her scarf around her neck, and tugged on her gloves. "I wouldn't miss it."

And with those enigmatic words, the landlady left Eliza and Silas.

"Well," Eliza said. "We've been told—something, I just don't know what."

"What have you done? Have you and Hyacinth been acting wild?"

"You needn't sound so hopeful," Eliza said. "I'm afraid we've done nothing more dangerous than shop for fabric, walk about Remembrance, and spend time at the Robbins home."

Unless, she realized as soon as she'd spoken, Mrs. Adams had heard about what had happened in St. Paul. But she'd never have been able to connect it with Eliza.

A thought leaped into her mind with such force that Eliza stopped suddenly, and Silas ran right into her. Guilt gnawed so deeply that it was beginning to erode her common sense.

The sole way out of letting Blaine Loring's vileness win was to fight back, and the only weapon she had was the truth.

A clean heart.

She knew what she had to do, and she was going to do it. The rhythmic coursing in her head began to fade as hope replaced it.

Eliza barely heard Silas's good-bye, scarcely registered

Hyacinth's chatter as they returned to the boardinghouse. Her mind was full of what she had to do, and her thoughts were racing to determine how to proceed.

She ate automatically as she mentally sorted through approaches to deal with her guilt, and at the end of the meal, Mrs. Adams reminded them to stay.

"I've come to a decision," the landlady announced. "It wasn't an easy one to make, but it's the right one. I have a daughter in Mankato, you know, and I'm going to move there to live with her."

"You have a daughter?" Eliza asked, coming out of her fog. The thought of Mrs. Adams having a family had never even crossed her mind.

"Yes, I have a daughter. And a son, too. He's in Minneapolis. But the point is that I'll be moving in with Ella and closing the boardinghouse."

"That's wonderful," Hyacinth said. "I mean that you're moving in with your daughter, not closing the boardinghouse. When is this going to happen?"

"In two weeks, if the weather holds. Ella and her husband will come up here and pack my belongings. I'll be living with them, so some of the furniture will be sold, I imagine."

The full import of what Mrs. Adams was saying sank in. Eliza would be without a home soon. Her stomach cramped at the thought.

Mrs. Adams crossed her arms over her broad chest and frowned. "Are you still planning then to take the old Lindstrom place?"

"The small house with the birdbath behind the store? Yes, when it's ready, which should be within a few days," Hyacinth answered. "I'll be leaving here and moving in there, so this should work out perfectly."

This couldn't be real. What was going to happen to her? Eliza's fingers curled into tight fists. Where could she go? Not back to St. Paul, certainly.

Hyacinth looked at Eliza. "If Eliza is willing, she can stay with me. We can be bachelor girls together."

Eliza sighed happily. *Thank You, Lord!* It was the answer to her prayer—or at least one of them.

This was the perfect solution, even if it was only temporary. Until she got things squared away in St. Paul, much of her life would be short-term solutions to long-term problems.

She heard only faintly the plans of the two older women to move some of the extra furniture from the boardinghouse into their new home. If but for a little while, she had some time.

Now she had to use it wisely.

❧

Silas blew out the lamp and stood at the window, staring toward the boardinghouse. Word had filtered back to him what Mrs. Adams wanted to talk to Eliza and Hyacinth about.

To be honest, he wouldn't miss the cantankerous landlady. Her stinginess was legendary in Remembrance. She could squeeze a penny and get a dollar, as Silas overheard one day in the general store, where apparently she'd taken the store owner to task for charging the same for two apples, when one was clearly larger than the other.

What was the matter with the world anyway? It seemed to get crazier every day. People couldn't stop fighting, and it escalated from arguing about the cost of an apple to major conflicts like the war that split the country in two just two decades ago.

If everybody would just learn the basic rules of conduct for life, things would go much easier. They weren't difficult.

The world was getting wilder, and it wasn't just the young people who were out of control. Older people were, too. One had only to look at Edward and Hyacinth to see a shining example of that. His parents raised him to know the rules and to obey them, and now, God rest their souls, their influence lived on.

He liked rules. They contained behavior, kept unruliness in check, and were, all in all, a superb way of ordering one's life.

But even he wasn't as bound by them as Mrs. Adams was. If she had her way, single people would spend each day in contemplation and prayer, with only two hours on Sunday for relaxation.

How was a fellow to court a girl with those rules?

Silas froze. *Undo that thought. Scratch it out.*

He didn't mean he would court a girl. Oh, not at all! He had better things to do than that. Professor Barkley addressed this repeatedly, so much so that Silas could quote him word for word. But just to be sure, he picked up the *Patented Five Year Plan for Success* and reread it: *A romantic entanglement is just that, an entanglement. It becomes a knot that cannot be loosened. Beware of such a thing. Look instead for a friendship, a good, deep friendship that runs as pure and true as an underground stream. That is to be valued. The Good Book says, "A friend loveth at all times."*

The Bible had always been a reliable set of rules. You couldn't top the Ten Commandments for clear regulations on how to live. Those commandments, added to *Thou shalt love the Lord thy God with all thy heart, and with all thy soul, and with all thy strength* summed up an outline for an ethical life.

Ethical and uncomplicated. Unfortunately they weren't the same. If everyone lived by the rules, life would be so much easier than it was now.

For one thing, his uncle wouldn't be marrying someone

he'd wooed across the country, someone with the improbable name of Hyacinth. What kind of name was Hyacinth anyway? What was wrong with a good solid name like Mary or Catherine or Sarah?

Or Eliza. He knew he was in dangerous territory with her. He was old enough to realize what was going on. He'd had girlfriends before, when he'd been a raw teenage boy. But now, it was different. He thought of her entirely too much, and lately he'd been revisiting their first meeting, when she had fallen into his arms, smelling of blueberries and soap.

She'd felt much too good in his arms. It would be easy to let his heart lead him right to her, to let himself go ahead and fall in love with her, but there was something in the way.

For one thing, he had too many unanswered questions about her life before she came here. Of course, he hadn't actually asked any of these questions, he had to admit, but maybe the time had come to do so.

He should make a list.

He padded over to the small table and found a pen and a piece of paper, and he sat down.

First order of business, he told himself, in making any list was to label it neatly. And so he did. QUESTIONS FOR MISS ELIZA DAVIS.

Already he felt better. He did like lists.

He continued, buoyed by knowing that this would help. He wrote the first question.

1. Why did you leave St. Paul?

She'd already told him a bit, but he needed more information. Moving, as he well knew, wasn't a process to be undertaken lightly. It was dreadful, all the sorting and packing, and then the actual move itself, followed by more unpacking and re-sorting. Nobody did it unless there was no other option. Eliza hadn't brought much with her—just that large carpetbag—but as far as he knew, maybe she didn't have any furniture to bring with her. Plus there was the awkward matter of the scoundrel that she'd had some kind of encounter with. He'd like to know more about that.

2. *Why did you come back to Remembrance?*

Again, she'd told him somewhat superficially, but he wanted more detail. She'd left here when she was a child. What were her memories of Remembrance that drew her back? He smiled, satisfied that this was an extraordinarily good question.

3. *Do you intend to stay in Remembrance? Why?*

That was actually two questions, but they needed each other.

4. *What makes you happiest? What has made you cry?*
   What do you need? Do you like me?

The last question slipped in, and he caught it before he wrote it down.

He carefully folded the paper and put it in his Bible. He'd take another look at it tomorrow.

Silas extinguished the lamp, knelt beside the bed, said his prayers of thanksgiving—Professor Barkley noted that one must always acknowledge all gifts—and moved on to his prayers of intercession. As always, the Robbins family was front and center. He didn't understand why God had done what He had done, but the Lord was sovereign and to be trusted.

His prayers for Eliza meandered off track into prayers that were more for him than her. She needed to stay—he needed her to stay. She needed to feel safe—he needed to reassure her. She needed to be loved—and he loved her.

If he hadn't been so tired, he might have fought the last one. But it sat right in his mind, a thought as warm and comfortable as hot cocoa. He let it stay.

He closed with requesting blessings on those near and far—he'd long ago figured that ought to cover everyone and everything—and got into bed.

A list. He had made a list. He smiled. This was the way to proceed. A list.

eight

"I hope that's all right with you," Hyacinth said to Eliza as they sat in the parlor of the boardinghouse. "It just came to me that it would work out for both of us, and you know how I am. My mind thinks it, and my mouth says it."

Eliza reached over and squeezed Hyacinth's hand. "You have no idea how much I appreciate it. When Mrs. Adams said she was closing the boardinghouse in two weeks, I thought I might end up homeless."

"Don't worry about that. I'd never let it happen." Hyacinth's eyes twinkled dangerously. "There's a young man in Remembrance who seems quite taken with you, and I'd like to see the two of you together."

Heat shot up Eliza's neck and into her face, and she knew she was blushing. "I don't think so."

"It would be wonderful. We could have a double wedding, and—"

"Oh, stop it!" Eliza interjected, laughing. "We're just friends."

Hyacinth nodded. "You are, and that's the best way to start a lifelong relationship. You need the basis of friendship—you need to like each other as well as love each other."

"Is that the way your marriage was?" Eliza asked softly.

"It was. He was my best friend, and I knew I could trust him with my heart. So I did."

"It must have been very hard when he died."

Tears filled Hyacinth's eyes. "Even now, it still hurts so bad that there are times I think I can't bear it. And when he died, and our son was so young, I didn't know how I could go on another day."

"But you did."

"I did. I had to. Thomas, our son, had to. We had to go on living even when my husband couldn't."

"You must be proud of your son."

"I am. When his father died, he took up the farm work. He was probably old enough by most people's standards—he was twelve—but he was my little boy. I wish you could have seen him, standing behind that big plow, trying to guide it through the packed earth while the patient horses walked just a bit slower, as if they knew that it wasn't Matthew behind the plow, but Thomas." Her eyes glowed with the memory.

"Might I ask another question?" Eliza ventured.

"You can ask. Until I hear the question, I don't know if I'll answer."

"What does your son think of you marrying Edward?"

"He has some hesitation, which I understand." Hyacinth smoothed the fabric of her dress over her lap, and a slight smile curved her lips. "Of course, no one is good enough for me in his mind. But he wants me to be happy, and he understands that, even though this hasn't been the most conventional courtship, it works for us."

A movement outside the window of the parlor caught Eliza's attention. "Silas is here." She clapped her hand over her mouth. "I wonder if he's expecting me to go to the Robbins house today."

"I want to go over there again," Hyacinth said. "Analia needs someone to brush her hair and fix it for her. And so does Mary Robbins. I'm not an expert at it, but I do like doing it."

"That would be wonderful! I know Analia really enjoyed

your 'lady time.' Mary's asked about you, too. Plus you'd get to see what's happening with the material you purchased. You'd be very welcome there."

"If Silas agrees. Honestly, sometimes I just don't know about that one."

As soon as Silas entered the parlor, with Mrs. Adams watchfully behind him, Hyacinth asked if she might go over.

"Absolutely," he said. "I was just there, as a matter of fact. The boys are having a heyday making swords out of leftover pieces of wood from the banister we replaced, and the poor little girl is stuck with a book in the corner, looking a bit overwhelmed. I don't think she's very interested in swords, and I suspect she'd like some female company."

Hyacinth stood up immediately. "I'll go over now."

"While you're there, Eliza and I will go check on the house where you'll be staying to see what's left to be done," Silas said.

"You mean Birdbath House?" Hyacinth asked with a wink at Eliza.

"Birdbath House?" Silas looked at them blankly. "It's the old Lindstrom place."

"The Lindstroms have been gone from Remembrance for almost seven years," Mrs. Adams said from the doorway.

"Then it shouldn't be called the old Lindstrom place, should it?" Eliza asked, joining in. "It should be called the new Mason place, or the Mason-Davis place."

"Or Birdbath House, since it has a birdbath." Hyacinth was buttoning her coat as she spoke.

"But what if the birdbath falls over, or is taken off the property?" Silas asked.

"Then it'll be the old Birdbath House, won't it?" Hyacinth chuckled. "Or Remembrance could give in and number the houses, and it'll be something as prosaic as 13 Oak Street."

Her laughter ringing behind her, Hyacinth swept out of the boardinghouse.

"It's not too cold outside," Silas said, "but it'll be cold at the house—Birdbath House, I guess I need to start calling it, although I've never heard of anything quite so silly. We'll need to check the stove and the fireplace while we're there to make sure nothing is blocked, no nests in the stovepipe or the flue."

Mrs. Adams cleared her throat. "I don't believe that a man and woman should be alone until they're married."

Silas sputtered wordlessly, and Eliza took his arm and smiled at the landlady. "We're only going to inspect and clean the house. Marriage hardly seems necessary for that."

Mrs. Adams stepped aside as they left, her disapproval following them out the door.

"I shouldn't have said that," Eliza said. "She means well."

"I imagine you'll be glad to leave there," Silas said as they headed out into the sunny afternoon. "It must be like living under a magnifying glass. She watches everything that you do."

"She does have definite ideas of right and wrong," Eliza said, loosening her muffler a bit. With the sun beaming overhead, the air seemed warm. "According to her, though, mostly everything is wrong. I appreciate the way she takes care of us, although I feel like a chicken that has hatched but the mother hen still insists on sitting on it."

He grinned. "What an image! I think she'd probably suffocate you."

"It feels like it sometimes."

The walk to the small house was short, and they were soon there.

The snow had begun to melt from the roof, and a steady

drip from the corner suggested that some repair might be necessary on the eaves. He opened the door for her.

It was definitely a small house. The rooms were tiny, with barely enough space to fit the dusty couch and the single wooden chair in the front room, and the two bedrooms each contained a small bed and bureau, which took up most of the space. The kitchen was oddly shaped, running along the entire back of the house, like a long narrow corridor.

"This was added on later," he said before she could ask the question. "If I'd built it, I believe I might have made it a foot or two wider, but what's done is done. I could take down this outer wall here, though, and expand this part."

Silas walked through the house, muttering about the changes that needed to be made.

The scent of old wallboards and wood smoke mingled with the slightly sour smell of a house that hadn't been aired out recently. The furniture had seen better days, to say the least. The textured tapestry of the sofa was worn in the shape of bodies that had sat in the same spot for years. Eliza ran her hand over the arm of the couch, and a tiny mouse scurried out from under the throw pillow.

"We will bring a cat in," Silas said, and she suppressed a smile at the little shiver of revulsion that he unsuccessfully hid. He looked for all the world as if he'd like to have fled from the room, back into the outdoors where mice crept and hid in bushes and rocks, not in the furniture.

"Not a fan of mice, are you?" she asked.

His laugh sounded a bit choked. "Who is? No, we'll bring in a cat."

"Can I keep it?"

"The mouse or the cat?"

Eliza had to grin. "The cat. Or will we be borrowing it?"

"There are enough barn cats in this neck of woods that I think we can accommodate you with a cat of your own. For a while, it was quite the booming industry, selling mousers to the townspeople, but nowadays, the farmers are just as happy to give you a kitten or two."

A cat. Eliza wanted to hug herself. She loved cats, but she hadn't had one since Tim and Hannah, the two she'd had when she lived in Remembrance. She gave them away when she left, and it broke her young girl's heart.

Now she'd have a cat again.

Silas was examining the stove. "It looks like it's been cleaned out, so I think it'll hold a good fire for you and Hyacinth." He looked doubtfully at the sofa. "Are you going to want to keep this furniture?"

She shook her head. One thing she knew for sure was that if she saw one mouse, there were another ninety-nine she didn't see. "I want to share the house with Hyacinth, not the rodents, and I suspect they've made their own homes in the furniture. We've already talked to Mrs. Adams about taking some of her furniture."

"Excellent idea." He grinned impishly. "And somehow I don't think that she allows mice in her house."

If the sofa was this bad, she could only imagine what shape the beds were in. The thought of mice living in the mattress beneath her would keep her from ever sleeping in this house. They'd undoubtedly burrowed their way in and made nests.

She shuddered at the thought. Yes, a much better idea was to jettison the furnishings that were there and replace them with ones from the boardinghouse.

"Hyacinth and I will talk to Mrs. Adams this afternoon about the furniture. Do you think you can bring in a cat as soon as possible?" A shadow darted along the corner of the room. "Preferably a hungry cat. A very big, very hungry cat."

"I know a fellow outside of town who's got just the creature for you. Big ugly thing."

"Who, the cat or the fellow?"

He laughed. "I meant the cat, but he's not much to look at either. Say, why don't you come with me? We can go now, and you can meet both of them—the man and the cat."

A ride in the country sounded wonderful, and soon they were both wrapped in thick blankets in his wagon, bouncing along the still-frozen ruts of the road out of Remembrance. "You'll like Carl," Silas said, speaking loudly over the creaks of the wheels. "He's a good Norwegian, a real honest sort. He doesn't come into town much, but every once in a while he'll show up at church or for a social or something."

Soon he pulled into a small farm, and a man in a thick jacket came out from the barn to greet them. "Howdy now," he said, his voice thickly accented with a Nordic lilt. "What brings you out today?"

"This is Eliza Davis," Silas said, "and she needs a cat. She's moving into the old Lindstrom place, and there are mice in it."

The large blond man nodded. *"Uff da."* Eliza didn't speak Norwegian, but she knew what that meant. It was the catchall phrase that roughly translated to *Oh my.* "Do you want to borrow Slick Tom, or do you want a kitten?"

"Slick Tom?" Eliza asked, and Carl nodded.

"I'll be right back." He disappeared into the barn and emerged a few minutes later with a gigantic yellow cat draped over his arm. "This is Slick Tom." The cat opened its eyes sleepily at the mention of its name.

One of Slick Tom's ears was half gone, and his back was striped with scars, visible through his scruffy fur. She reached out and touched his head, and the cat produced a purr that must have been audible the next farmyard over.

"He's wonderful," she murmured.

"Yah, he is a good mouser," Carl said. "I'll send him back with you, and he'll have the place cleared out in two days. You might want to get a kitten, too, though. All the kits are from Slick Tom, so they've got his talent." He handed Slick Tom to Silas, who looked as if he'd just been given a crocodile.

Carl grinned at Eliza. "Silas ain't much for cats."

"His loss," she said, hiding her amusement as best she could when Slick Tom stuck his gigantic head under Silas's chin and sighed with pleasure.

Again Carl went into the barn, and this time he came out with a gray-striped kitten. "This is a girl. She'll be a good hunter. You can tell by the ears, you know."

"Of course," she murmured, although she had no idea what that meant. She was too enchanted with the kitten that curled up against her chest.

"Your good mousers will have large ears," Carl explained. "Helps them hear the mice. Now here's what you do. Put them both in the house. Slick Tom knows what to do, and by the time he's got all the mice out, this little gray will have learned from him. Bring him back, and you can keep the girl."

Silas helped her into the wagon and handed her Slick Tom. Immediately the oversized cat curled up into a ball on her lap while the kitten chewed on the button of her coat.

Two cats on her lap, and Silas at her side. Life was lovely.

❧

Silas opened the door of Birdbath House. Twilight had crept early across the land, and the hard chill of the night was settling in.

"Here, kitty-kitty-kitty," he called, feeling like an idiot. But one couldn't exactly talk to a cat like one would to, say, a business associate. He tried it. "Good evening, Mr. Slick Tom and Miss, I'm sorry I didn't catch your name earlier. Has the day been profitable?"

He lit the lamp that was on the table, and a circle of light illuminated the room. "Oh, I shouldn't have done that."

The day's catch was laid out in a tidy line with the two cats, the big yellow one and the little gray one, sitting proudly beside the row. He patted each cat awkwardly on the head, told them each what good hunters they were, and left them to their spoils. He'd check the next day to make sure the harvest was taken care of before bringing Eliza over.

Eliza. How easily—and how completely—she had moved into his life. She was a complication he never foresaw, despite Professor Barkley's warnings about being prepared for the unexpected.

What would he have done if he had known she was coming into his life? What if he *had* been able to expect the unexpected?

He shook his head. Much more thinking like this, and he'd be as loony as his uncle.

Love was what it was. There was no use complicating it by trying to figure out the *how* or the *why*. Just the *who* was enough.

Suddenly Slick Tom sailed through the air and pounced on something. As the cat came back, the prize dangling in his mouth, Silas decided he'd continue this train of thought in the safety of his own rodent-free home.

Until Slick Tom finished the job here, Silas knew he wouldn't be lingering at Birdbath House.

❧

Eliza watched Silas as he read. They were waiting for Hyacinth and Edward to return from a short walk. Edward rarely used the cane, and soon he wouldn't need it at all.

Silas had picked up a treatise on the properties of knowledge. It seemed too thin to cover the topic at all well, but she kept that to herself.

He'd offered her a newspaper, or another book, but she refused. What she needed to say would make concentration impossible.

"Silas," she said, twisting in the seat uncomfortably, "I need to talk to you." She clenched her fingers around the arms of the chair, not to keep her on the slippery cushion but to keep her from fleeing the house.

He raised his head from his book and slowly focused on her. She'd come to anticipate that expression with delight. He had the ability to completely immerse himself in whatever he read, and he moved so slowly into the world of reality.

"Yes?" He took his wire-rimmed glasses off.

"I have to—" She stopped. "I must— I need to—"

He smiled slightly. "Then by all means, you should."

"When I was in St. Paul, I knew Blaine Loring." The words sprang out.

"Blaine Loring?" He put his glasses back on, as if they helped him understand her better. "The name is somewhat familiar, but I can't place it right now."

God, help me, please. Obviously she'd need some divine help if she were to tell him the whole sordid story.

She squeezed the arms of the chair even tighter. "He's the man that Edward read about from the paper. He took money from young women in St. Paul, claiming he was going to invest it for them, when in fact, he didn't."

Silas's brow wrinkled with concern. "Oh, Eliza, he took advantage of you, too? I was afraid of that."

"Well, yes." This was not getting any easier.

"How much did you lose?"

She lowered her head. "I didn't lose any money," she whispered at last, the hand of guilt wrapped firmly around her heart.

"I don't understand."

Eliza swallowed hard. There was nothing to do at this stage but to barrel on through. "I thought Blaine and I were in love. He could charm the wool off a sheep."

"The wool off a sheep?" he asked blankly.

"It's a phrase my father used to describe someone who could talk people out of whatever he wanted. That was Blaine Loring. His 'love' for me was only a cover."

Silas's lips thinned to a hard line. "Are you telling me that Loring took liberties with you? That he abused your innocence?"

Eliza's face flushed even hotter. "No! Not that! I mean that he saw in me someone who could help him with his snake oil plan. He made me think that he loved me, and I was so gullible that I believed him."

"Eliza," Silas said, leaning closer, "we should thank God that you weren't prey to his swindle. I'm sure that you weren't the only one he charmed."

"Probably. But I might be the only one who helped him with his con game." She put her head in her hands.

"You helped him? How?" Disbelief rang in his voice.

She wanted to get up, to run from this house, to leave Remembrance. This had been a terrible, terrible idea.

"I was the go-between. I convinced the other women in service to the wealthy families in St. Paul to give their money to him. He had a plan, he said, that would let them double, triple, maybe quadruple what they'd given him."

"How much money—how many of these women are we talking about?"

Eliza blinked back the tears that stung her eyes. "I don't know how much money. How many women did I bring to this? Twenty-five, maybe thirty."

She didn't want to revive the memory of how she'd taken advantage of these women for him, how she sacrificed their friendships. He changed her enough that she stopped seeing them as friends. Instead, they'd all become investors. That made him happy—and she recreated her life just to keep him happy.

"What did you tell them?" he asked stiffly. "Did you tell them that investments aren't sure things?"

"No. I told them there was no risk at all. That's what he told me, and that's what I told them." Her stomach twisted. "How could I have been so foolish?"

"And what did he promise you? Some of the money? A cut of the profits?"

"No! I did it because I thought we'd be together. I did it because I thought I loved him. I did it because I thought he loved me." Her voice caught in a sob.

Silas was silent. The ticking of the clock on the mantel was the only sound.

"Do you see what I've done?" she asked him, the words ragged as she tried to talk around the pain. "I helped him. I did. And—God forgive me—I hurt my friends. And what do I have left? Only guilt."

Her fingers gripped the arms of the chair. "I don't know much about the law, but I suspect that what he did was illegal. Silas, do you see? I helped him. I helped him! That makes me an accomplice."

He stared past her, his face a stony mask.

"Say something," she begged.

He stood up and turned to leave the room.

"Please. You must say something." She knew she was pleading, but it meant so much to her. "Say you hate me. Say I disgust you. Say—please say you forgive me."

He stopped. When he spoke, he was still facing the door, not her. "I don't hate you. I don't find you disgusting. I have one question for you, though."

"What is it?"

"If you believed him, if you thought what you offered your friends was a true investment, why didn't you invest in it, too?"

Her breath froze in her chest. Why, indeed, hadn't she? The answer was too horrible to consider.

He left the room. She was left alone by the fireplace, but she was colder than she could ever have imagined. Even the flames burning behind the hearth couldn't warm the iciness that had enclosed her heart with his final words.

She stood up, got her wrap from the coat tree by the front door, and let herself out. The sun was shining brightly, and the winter birds were singing, but she was only vaguely aware of them.

When she'd come to Remembrance, she'd run away from everything associated with Blaine Loring—or so she thought. But she hadn't been able to escape the stain that was on her soul.

She needed somebody to forgive her. Silas? God? Herself?

❧

"So I've got my eye on the ruby ring I saw advertised in the Duluth paper," Edward said at the dinner table. "I think Hyacinth would like it, don't you?"

"Yes." Silas shoved the piece of potato through the gravy on his plate until it came apart.

"I'd like to go to Duluth fairly soon to look at it. Would you like to go?"

"Yes." A green bean began to make the same trip through the gravy.

"Good. And we'll look into getting a panda as a pet and riding grasshoppers onto the moon."

"That would be fine."

"Silas, would you pay attention? You haven't heard a word I've said, have you?" Edward frowned at his nephew.

"I heard," Silas protested. "A ring, Duluth, and—oh, I don't know. Sorry, I wasn't focusing."

"What's wrong? You've been in a slump all evening."

Silas shoved his plate away. The dinner was undoubtedly tasty, but it all sat like dry cardboard in his mouth. "Guess I'm not hungry."

"Guess you're in love."

"In love? With whom?" Silas glared at his uncle. Truly he had lost his mind. Eliza was—well, she was Eliza.

His uncle smiled. "I'd say that Eliza Davis has done a job on your heart."

Silas snorted. "You are mistaken. Eliza has done nothing to my heart, nothing at all."

"Love doesn't have to be this painful experience you're making it out to be. Let yourself enjoy it."

"The way you are?" Silas snapped. "You and Hyacinth? Are you insane?"

Uncle Edward nodded happily. "Yes, indeed. Insane with love."

"I don't believe you're saying this." Silas pushed his chair away from the table so furiously that it fell over. "Just because you and Hyacinth act like a couple of moonstruck youngsters doesn't mean that everyone has to be in love. I'm not in love with Eliza. Not at all."

He slammed his napkin onto the table and stalked out of the dining room.

In love with Eliza. What an inane thing to say. How could he love someone who had participated in such a blackguardly deal as she did, bilking young women out of their savings? Here he'd thought she was innocent, when in fact she was completely the opposite.

He went up to his bedroom, the only place in the house where he was guaranteed a modicum of privacy.

In love with Eliza. Humph.

Some time with the Word might settle his spirit. He sat at his table and opened his Bible, and as he did so, a piece of blue paper fluttered to the ground.

It was the list. What a silly piece of business that had been. He was such a fool to have been taken in by her.

Had it been just yesterday that he'd written it? He couldn't stop himself from unfolding the list and rereading it.

Why did you leave St. Paul? He didn't need to ask that question anymore. He had the answer.

Why did you come back to Remembrance? He could figure that one out on his own. She was running, trying to escape the proverbial long arm of the law.

Do you intend to stay in Remembrance? Why? Again, that had become quite clear. Remembrance was a tiny dot on a map. No one would think to look for her here.

What makes you happiest? What has made you cry? What do you need? He didn't even want to know the answers to these questions, but they answered themselves anyway. Swindling people made her happy. Getting caught made her cry. She needed someone to hide her.

Then there was the question he hadn't written on the paper,

only in his mind. *Do you like me?*

He buried his face in his hands.

Why had God done this to him? Why had God let him fall in love with a criminal?

His pulse hammered in his temples. No, no, no.

He had just admitted it to himself. He was in love with her. Despite the litany of reasons he shouldn't love her, he did. It made the pain that much worse.

Darkness washed into his room, and still he sat at the table, stricken by the realization—and the nasty corollary that came with it. He loved her, and he couldn't. He could not love someone who was as morally flawed as she was.

So this was what heartache was, he thought almost detachedly. No wonder the poets wrote of it and the musicians sang of it.

What was he to do? Professor Barkley hadn't dealt with this, but he also repeatedly warned against the knotty experience of love. There was no point in consulting the *Five Year Plan* to see what counsel the professor would give.

He opened his Bible and found the comfort verse of the Lord's Prayer in the book of Matthew. The triumph of the last lines, *For thine is the kingdom, and the power, and the glory, for ever*, never failed to elevate his mood. That was the promise of the prayer.

With a start, he noticed the two verses that follow the Lord's Prayer: *For if ye forgive men their trespasses, your heavenly Father will also forgive you: But if ye forgive not men their trespasses, neither will your Father forgive your trespasses.*

How could he have missed the lines before? It was as if God was speaking directly to him, pointing out the divinity of forgiveness, and the necessity of the act of forgiveness.

He had refused to forgive Eliza. Clearly he was wrong.

He recalled the words of the sermon Reverend Tupper had preached. Forgiveness was the first step to renewing the relationship between God and himself, to restore the bond of Creator and creation. Now it was his turn to work on his own "clean heart."

And it was time to start learning how to love.

nine

"We're all going to the Robbins's house today," Hyacinth announced the next morning at breakfast. "Eliza, dear, are you sure you're not sick? Your eyes are bloodshot."

"I'll be fine. I can't guarantee how straight my seams will be, though." Eliza manufactured a smile. The last thing she wanted to do was to be around Silas, but Analia's striped dress was so close to being done that she could probably finish it today.

She had no choice. She had to go.

Actually it was probably not going to be a problem anyway. The way Silas had walked from her, oozing disapproval, meant that he probably would manage to stay as far away from her as he could.

"We're meeting at Edward and Silas's house," Hyacinth continued. "Edward wants to show me something." She leaned over and in a conspiratorial whisper said, "I think it's a ring."

Eliza mustered up all the enthusiasm she could. Even if her life had fallen into shreds, she needed to be upbeat about her friend's romance. "Did he get it? What does it look like?"

"I don't think he has it yet. We'll see when we get over there."

I don't want to do this. I don't want to do this. I don't want to do this. The silent words echoed through Eliza's mind as she and Hyacinth walked over to the Collier house.

Edward sat by the window, his ever-present Duluth newspaper in his hands, but this time it was folded open to a

116

particular page. "Hyacinth, my morning flower!"

Silas looked at the ceiling and rolled his eyes as he mouthed, *My morning flower?*

Edward was showing Hyacinth an advertisement in the paper. "Do you like it?" he asked, and in response got a loud kiss from her. He winked at Eliza. "I guess she does!"

Hyacinth danced over to Eliza and held the paper out. "Look at this ring! Isn't it beautiful? It's to be my wedding ring!"

It was indeed a lovely ring, but Eliza's eyes were riveted on the story beside the advertisement. It was a short news story, stating simply that without further evidence, the case against Blaine Loring would be dropped.

Had Silas seen it? She must know.

"Let's leave the lovebirds alone for a moment," she suggested to him. "I'd like some tea before we go to the Robbins house."

"Of course." Silas looked confused but followed her into the kitchen.

"Did you read the paper?" she asked without preamble as he put some water on to boil.

"My uncle showed me the advertisement for the ring if that's what you mean. Why, do you think that she really won't like it?"

Eliza shook her head vigorously. "Not the ring. It's beautiful, and she'll wear it proudly. No, I mean the story next to it."

"I guess I was too busy watching Uncle Edward extol the virtues of the ring. Why?"

"The case against Blaine is going to be dropped for lack of evidence."

He froze. "That would be a good thing for you," he said, overly polite. "It lets you off."

"No, it's not a good thing for anyone. I wasn't part of this, not knowingly at any rate. You have to believe me. I want him to go to jail for what he did. If he isn't prosecuted, he'll do it again."

He had to believe her, had to understand what happened. He had no idea the pain she was in, how it was eating at her.

"So what do you intend to do about it?" He measured tea into a strainer and laid it over a cup.

"What can I do?" She clutched his arm. "Really, Silas, what can I do?"

"You could provide a statement."

She shook her head. "I've already thought of that, but it won't work. St. Paul isn't like Remembrance. No one is going to believe me. I'm just the voice of a young workingwoman, one who has been spurned, no less. Do you think my testimony would carry any weight?"

"So what's your solution, then? Either you do something, or you don't."

"It's not that simple."

"Isn't it?"

He picked up a pencil and one of his uncle's old newspapers, and in large strokes, drew a square. In it he wrote PROBLEM. Under it he added two slanting lines, labeled DO SOMETHING and DO NOTHING.

"But do what?" she asked impatiently. Sometimes he was so analytical that he couldn't see that reality and logic were often on two different planes entirely.

"You go to the police. You tell them what you know, and justice will take its due course." He spoke plainly and flatly, as if he were explaining it to a child.

"You're a man, Silas, a man with some status. You're respected for your gender and your career at the very least. I'm a woman, a seamstress, and as if that weren't bad enough, he rejected me. I'm the cast-off woman, so whatever I say will be dismissed as my attempt at retribution."

"Really, Eliza. You've certainly got this thought through." His voice was cold.

"Don't you understand that you could tell the police what happened, and you'd be believed? I doubt that I would. Think about it, Silas. Think about it!"

"You want me to testify for you?"

Oh, he was so maddening. "No, I don't."

The teakettle whistled, and he took it off the flame and poured the water over the tea in the strainer. "Eliza, it really is as simple as I've shown you. Now you have to decide which of these"—he moved the teacup aside and ran his finger over the diagram—"you will do."

There was no point in going further with him. Any discussion simply cemented his concept of her as being a willing participant in the sordid situation.

"You're right," she said. She picked the cup from the table and swirled the steaming tea in it, anything to keep him from seeing how badly her hands were shaking. She couldn't bear to look at him. If he saw the hot anger in her eyes, he'd once again misinterpret it.

All she'd wanted was support from him. That's what friends did. Was it too much to ask of him? Apparently so. She'd failed whatever test of logic and reasoning he'd set up, and that failure was enough for him to sever their friendship.

What he hadn't bargained for, though, was that by his very actions, he failed her test—her test of friendship, of caring, of love.

She gulped the tea, ignoring the burning path it seared in her mouth and throat. This was the least of her concerns.

"I'm ready to leave now."

As she began to step out of the kitchen, he put a restraining hand on her arm. "Wait. I don't think we've finished here."

"Oh, we've finished. I have nothing more to say. Now I will go to do what I know how to do—sew. I am going to stitch down seams and make buttonholes in five shirts and hem a dress. I will do it well, and I will do it now, because I am leaving."

"I don't mean to—" He held out his hand as if to stop her.

"I don't care. Maybe I will care tonight and maybe I will tomorrow, but right now I don't. You let me down. I wanted you to be there for me, to listen, to help me see my way through this mess, but you don't want to hear anything except your simplistic little diagram." She strode back into the room and seized it from the table and shook it in front of him. "Two lines. That's all. Two lines. Do you really think life is made that way? Two lines? Two completely straight lines?"

She could hear herself. She was out of control, raging at him. He stared at her, his astonishment so clear it might as well have been written on his face.

She couldn't stop. "The crux of the matter here is that I needed you, and you not only refused to support me, you turned away. Even if you think I am the worst sinner in the world, even if my soul is stained so badly that it reeks of transgression, who are you to dismiss me?" Tears crowded into her eyes. "I thought we were friends. I thought we were—"

In one step, he had her in his arms, his lips buried in her hair, half-kissing, half-murmuring reassurances. She leaned against him, knowing that the tears, which were now flowing freely, were soaking into his shirt. He smelled of clean cotton, a bit of wood smoke, and shaving cream. He smelled of strength.

Their words tumbled over each other's until they could no

longer tell which one was speaking.

"I'm sorry. . .always. . .forever. . .love you."

She'd needed this. Tenderness wasn't Blaine Loring's style, to say the least.

But being held by Silas was comforting, and his energy flowed into her.

How long had it been since she'd felt this safe, this protected? She didn't want to move. If she could stay right where she was, enclosed in Silas's embrace, the world could spin on in its crazy course, and it wouldn't touch her.

A chorus of less-than-subtle coughs from the doorway told her they weren't alone. She and Silas sprang apart quickly.

"Now there are a couple of guilty looking mugs," Edward said, grinning.

"Guilty? I'd say happy." Hyacinth beamed at them both.

Eliza glanced at Silas. His face was bright red. "We need to get to the Robbins house," he said almost gruffly, without even a glance at Eliza.

The feeling of well-being evaporated. The moment of tenderness was short-lived, and he was back to being distant.

"We're going to have to have a talk, you and I," Edward said, putting his arm around his nephew as they headed for the door. "You're missing something here, something pretty important."

Hyacinth hung back and let the men leave the room. Then she looped her arm through Eliza's. "Men," she said in a conspiratorial whisper. "Some of them are like horses."

"Horses?" Eliza stared at her friend. "What are you talking about?"

"You have to train a horse," Hyacinth said, "and you have to train a man, too. My Matthew was just like Silas at the beginning. He had an incredible mind for the business of running the farm. He knew where every penny went. Nothing escaped him. Nothing except how to love."

"But shouldn't it come naturally?"

"Honey, Matthew loved me. I never had a moment's doubt about that, but he wasn't good at all with understanding that love is like a busy city street. Traffic goes both ways. To him, and from him. To me, and from me. Once he learned that I needed love from him, and I don't just mean kissing and hugging—I mean the special look over a shared memory, or a wildflower picked because he knew I'd like it, or making a cup of tea for me without my having to ask for it—then our marriage became extraordinary."

"I can't train Silas. The fact is, he isn't a horse. What do I do, tempt him with a handful of oats?"

Hyacinth laughed. "Now that I'd like to see. Eliza, you're misunderstanding me. Silas's heart isn't prepared for love. I think he's been completely blindsided by you. His heart will have to soften to let you into it. Right now he's resisting loving you. It couldn't be more obvious if he plastered a sign on the door of the mercantile. When I say you need to train him, I mean you need to help him open his heart so that the two of you can have the greatest love possible."

Eliza put her hands over her ears. "Stop! I can't change Silas. You know what he's like. You might as well be telling me to flap my arms and fly to the moon."

"I know it seems that way, but you can do it."

Eliza shook her head. "I don't want to. You're presuming I want Silas to love me. Well, I don't. I don't love him, and he doesn't love me."

"Eliza, that's not true."

She couldn't tell anymore. Her heart had been so battered with Blaine Loring that she thought it might never recover.

Just minutes ago, Silas had held her tightly and said something about love—and then promptly rejected her again.

Hyacinth sighed. "Young love. It's never easy."

"It's not love. Haven't you watched him around me? He doesn't love me."

"Oh, I've watched both of you, and he does love you. He's sneaky about it, and he doesn't let you see it, and he's fighting it with everything he's got and whatever else he can borrow, but he's smitten."

Eliza shook her head. "You're seeing what you want to see. You're in love with Edward, and you want Silas and me to be in love."

"I do like a good love story," Hyacinth said, "and I'm a sap for a happy ending."

A good love story and a happy ending. Both seemed impossible.

"We'd better get going," Eliza said. "Buttonholes await."

❧

There was no need to think about anything at the Robbins house, Silas thought. To tell the truth, there was no way to think, not with the chaos of six children eddying around him. Today they seemed especially rambunctious.

He'd put his hammer down to pick up the try square. The top of the cupboard seemed a bit off, and he wanted to make sure it was straight. He'd put the try square out of the reach of the children, who found the metal and rosewood tool to be fascinating. When he returned the try square to the toolbox and reached again for the hammer, it was gone, taken by a curious boy who was pounding a large nail into the middle of the board that was to be the center of the cupboard door.

Only by the grace of God had he not lost his temper. The board had been rendered unusable by the nail protruding from it, and he'd dug through the other pieces of wood to see if something else would work, and of course, he hadn't found a thing.

Now he rocked back on his heels, studying the partially assembled door and trying to figure out how to redeem the thing. He'd had the whole thing planned out, with every detail laid out so that no wood was wasted. Now not only was an expensive piece of wood wasted, but he'd have to buy more, and it wouldn't match. . . .

This was frustrating.

He was trying to help, but there were so many impediments. No wonder Jack hadn't been able to keep up with the household repairs. Who could?

A small arm snaked around his shoulders, and a sticky mouth pressed against his cheek. "It's a pretty door," little Mark said, his two-year-old body leaning against Silas's. "When I grow up, I want to be a wood-pounder like you."

His anger evaporated. A wood-pounder!

"You'll be a great wood-pounder," he said, hugging the boy back.

"Do you like my shirt?" Mark asked, puffing his chest out as much as he could. "Miss Davis just finished it, and she said I look very handsome indeed."

Silas glanced up, but Eliza was bent over another shirt, her bottom lip caught in her teeth as she worked. The sunlight caught a light reddish tinge of her hair, making it almost bronze. A single lock of hair had escaped the coiled bun at the back of her neck, and she pushed it out of the way, only to have it fall right back down again.

"Miss Davis knows fashion," Silas said, "so if she said you're very handsome in the shirt, then, my man, you are."

"I'm going to show my mother," the boy said, and with one

last admiring look at the cupboard door, he darted off.

The boy certainly was a charmer, and he was obviously delighted with his new shirt. Silas peeked at Eliza again. She was sewing a button on a shirt that was a larger copy of Mark's. What a blessing she had been to this family.

He wasn't going to think about her now. He couldn't. For one thing, he needed to solve the puzzle of the wood.

Silas studied the wood laid out before him, trying to see if there was any solution to the problem. But he had planned precisely, and losing the big piece in the middle meant that it couldn't be done.

"Silas!" His uncle's voice boomed across the room.

"Uncle Edward?" He stood up, wincing as he realized his foot had gone to sleep. "What are you doing here?"

"I've got cabin fever. In case you hadn't noticed, my boy, this has been a long winter. My foot is almost healed, and I felt like a walk. So I thought I'd come over and see if I could help."

"Hyacinth is with Mrs. Robbins. Little Mark just ran in to show her his new shirt that Eliza made."

Uncle Edward picked his way carefully over to Silas's side. "You've got a lot of projects going on at once. Not being critical here, just commenting. . ."

"It's true." Silas moved the stack of wood aside to make a path for his uncle. "I'm doing the cupboard now. It'll go right over here by the window."

"You trued it, didn't you?" Uncle Edward looked at the partially assembled piece. "It looks perfectly square."

"I put the try square on it again just a bit ago. I wanted to make sure it was perfect before I went any further."

"Excellent."

Uncle Edward's words meant much to Silas. He took great

pride in his carpentry, and in the past months he'd taught Silas to do the same, even if it meant taking longer in the preparation.

"I do have a problem." Silas held up the board with the nail sticking out of it.

His uncle laughed. "I don't believe I've ever seen woodworking quite like that. Whatever possessed you to do that?"

"I can't take credit for it. I suspect one of the younger carpenters—or wood-pounders, as Mark calls us—is responsible. Here's the situation: I have exactly enough wood, and my plan was—"

He explained it to his uncle, and when he had finished, he watched his uncle mentally analyze the dilemma.

"Hand me a pencil and paper," Uncle Edward said at last. "How about if you do this, and this, and this. You can lay the wood in at an angle. It's going to be more work, and you'll have to make sure you get the angle exactly the same on each piece, but you can do it if you use the miter square." He picked up the tool, like the try square but with the rosewood piece set at a slant. "It'll actually be very intriguing if you do it this way."

Uncle Edward was right. It was even more striking when the wood was placed in the door in an angular pattern. Still, he looked at his own plans, with the long slabs of wood placed in strict vertical lines, and he hated to let them go. But he had no choice.

He thanked his uncle, who stayed and watched and advised for a while before touring the rest of the house with Jack Robbins. Silas worked carefully and efficiently, and by the end of the afternoon, when night had stolen the daylight from the room, he lifted the finished piece into place.

"I like the design," Eliza said, as she came over to examine the new cupboard. "I know you had to change it, but it worked out."

"It did, didn't it?"

"Edward and Hyacinth have already left. I hope you don't mind walking with me." Was it his imagination, or did she stumble over the sentence?

"I don't mind." He hated the way the words came out, stiff and unwieldy.

They left the Robbins house and made their way without speaking to the boardinghouse. The silence was so heavy it was choking. He made an attempt at small talk. "When do you plan to move into the house?"

"Mrs. Adams hopes to leave in a week, so we will probably go in three or four days, depending on when her children arrive. Her daughter and her husband and her son will all be here to help her. They'll move the furniture we're taking into the house."

"And the cat?"

"Tiger is spending her days in the house, catching whatever mice might be bold enough to come in, although the Robbins children really like it when she comes with me. They must tucker her out pretty good. Whenever I go to leave, she's in with Mary, sound asleep."

He laughed. "Six children wear me out!"

"If she spends the day at Birdbath House, we go over at night and bring her to the boardinghouse. Mrs. Adams was fine with that, which surprised me. She told us initially that we couldn't have animals in the house. I believe her exact words were, 'No animals, not a cat, not a dog, not a chicken.'"

"A chicken?"

"I didn't ask. Well, maybe she's just ready to leave and that's why she lets Tiger stay."

"Maybe. Would you like to get the cat now? It'll save you an extra trip this evening." *And it'll give me more time with you*, he added mentally. Maybe he'd find a way to talk to her without sounding as if he'd been dipped in wax.

"If you don't mind, that would be wonderful."

Birdbath House was deeply shadowed, but the little cat was easy to find. She was waiting at the door for them and mewed when she saw Eliza. Eliza swept the kitten up and tucked her into her scarf. "I think she's hungry. Mrs. Adams saves her scraps of meat, and Tiger has become quite a fan of her cooking. I'd always heard that a cat won't mouse if it's fed, but apparently that's not true. Mrs. Adams told me that, and of course she's right."

He reached for the doorknob as she turned, and they met, their faces only inches apart. Automatically he put his hands on her shoulders to steady her, and for a moment, he couldn't move.

His silly chart that he had drawn out earlier reappeared in his mind, only this time in the box was written: *KISS HER?* and from the bottom of it came two lines. One said *YES*, and one said *NO*.

His words came back to haunt him. It was simple, he had said. One path or the other.

Her eyes were deep blue in the faint light of the dying moon, and her lips were open just a bit.

He could kiss her. He wanted to, so very badly. But was it the right thing to do?

The image of that inane diagram flashed in front of him again. Yes? No? He chose, and he leaned forward, and she leaned forward, until their lips were almost touching. Suddenly with a flash of fur and tiny sharp claws, the cat squeezed free from between them, hissed angrily at him, and shot onto Eliza's shoulder.

"Who knew our chaperone would be so small?" she said, laughing somewhat shakily.

"And so effective." He touched her chin where Tiger had dug her claws in while making her getaway. "I think you're bleeding."

"Oh, great. Well, Silas, I do believe this is our cue to leave." She stepped back and peeled the cat from her shoulder and tucked her again into her scarf. "I need to get to the boardinghouse before Tiger here decides to eat my ear off or something."

"Eliza, we need to talk."

"Not now," she said, opening the door and stepping out into the winter night. "I'm not ready, and neither are you. We both have some deep praying to do. Today our emotions did our thinking. Maybe after we've had some food and some sleep and some prayer, we'll be able to use our brains, too."

He could only nod.

They didn't speak again until they came to the steps of the boardinghouse.

"Eliza," he said, clutching his hands together so they wouldn't reach out for her, "I meant it."

She stopped. "Meant what?"

"I meant it when I said I love you."

And with those words, he turned and walked away.

He knew what he had to do. He had to quit trying to figure it out, trying to justify it, or even trying to make sense of it all—whatever "it" was. Instead he needed to trust in the Lord and let his heart be open to His will.

Love was like the cupboard. He had his plan, his plan

didn't work, and he found out that there was another plan that was even better than his. If it worked with cupboards, why wouldn't it work with love?

In his tired mind, it made sense.

ten

He loved her, did he? Could life become any more confused?

Eliza sat down at the table in her room and tried to think it through. If she was going to let herself fall in love with Silas—*as if that ship hadn't already sailed,* she added wryly—she was going to have to do something about the situation with Blaine Loring.

She slammed her fist on the table so hard that Tiger woke from her catnap with a start. She reached over and reassured the kitten, which promptly fell back asleep. It wasn't fair. She shouldn't have to still be dealing with the leftovers from that horrid situation. She should be done with it.

She was completely blameless, after all. She'd had no idea what he'd been doing with his nefarious plan.

Or had she?

She forced herself to revisit the earlier days of their romance, when he told her about his investment business. If it was a success, he'd be rich. She would have a fine house, lovely clothes, the chance to travel around the world.

Eliza rubbed her forehead with her fingertips as if she could erase those images. She'd been so young then, so innocent, so guileless. She'd been only a pawn in his evil business, drawn in by his alluring promises.

Suddenly she sat up as she realized the truth. She had to have known, but she'd managed to lie to herself, too. She wasn't stupid. She'd known, even then, that the money couldn't go in that many directions. The dollars that the nannies and cooks gave her couldn't make them and Blaine and her wealthy. Promises? No, lies.

She'd told herself she believed them because she wanted to, she had to. If she'd acknowledged the truth, that he was a crook, she would have had to commit to a life of thievery and deceit or give up Blaine Loring.

She had known, and she had continued.

Silas had seen it immediately. The day she poured out her heart to him, confessing her involvement with Blaine's scheme, he said he had one question for her—why hadn't she invested, too?

Was she stupid? Ignorant? Or had she purposely looked the other way? On some level, she'd known.

The realization was dreadful.

Her heart ached as she took in the consequences of the choice she'd made. So many lives had been hurt, so many dreams shattered and yet he was going to walk away, with no penalty of any kind. *Why would he?* she asked herself bitterly. The women had paid the price already.

She took out a sheet of paper and a pencil, and redrew the diagram Silas had made. PROBLEM? And then, DO NOTHING and DO SOMETHING.

She stared at what she had drawn. DO NOTHING. DO SOMETHING. Did she really have any choice?

She slashed an *X* through DO NOTHING and penned a circle around DO SOMETHING. The choice was made.

The time had come to take back her life, to rid herself of Blaine Loring's specter forever. She would go back to St. Paul.

There was time to catch the train through Remembrance. She still had some cash with her, though it was running low, and it should be enough to get her to the city again. She'd have to pack quickly, though.

She took her bag from the bottom of the armoire and

opened it, getting ready to place into it two or three of her nicer dresses. The ivory wool was probably the best to wear before the police. It was a copy of one she'd made for the wife of a wealthy retailer, and it looked elegantly respectable.

She took the jacket off the hanger and folded it carefully. She wouldn't have time to steam it out later. As she opened the case wider to put the jacket in, she noticed a piece of paper sticking out from the bottom section of the bag.

She pulled it out, and her fingers trembled as she recognized Blaine's handwriting. She scanned through it and recognized what it was.

It was the list of investors she'd gone to deliver that fateful night in St. Paul. She'd been so horrified at the sight of him with another woman that she ran back home without giving it to him. Then she packed so quickly that she must have mindlessly put it in the bag.

She sat down and looked at what she held in her hands. It was more than a list of investors. It was a roster of all the women who had invested in his plan, with the amount they'd given him. According to the document, a ship was due to arrive in the Great Lakes with a cargo of fine porcelain, and the women as investors were owners of the contents, which would be sold at a great profit in Duluth.

There was something terribly wrong with that list. She studied it and read through it again and again, trying to decode what the problem was.

The names and numbers swam in front of her eyes until they quit making any sense at all.

14%
19%
17%

21%
15%
8%
13%
11%
20%

It just didn't add up. How could that be? Just that single column—and there were more—added up to 138 percent. There couldn't be 138 percent.

She must have added wrong. She checked her totals again. Still, the numbers added up to 138 percent. But the largest it could be was 100 percent.

There was only one delivery of porcelain that he sold portions to. All the women invested in the same shipment. It was like a bad mathematics problem but this time, she understood. It meant that—

She froze as she realized what he had done. He hadn't just stolen the money. No, this was more elaborate than that.

Fortunately his ego had been bigger than his brain, and he wrote everything down, probably so he could look at the numbers and enjoy how he outsmarted the women. He was such a small, little man, she realized. So small.

But his beautifully formatted list told the story that the police would want to hear. If they wouldn't listen to her, maybe they would listen to Blaine Loring himself—or at least his handwritten columns of proof.

She added together all the numbers, and found that in the end, he had promised nearly 350 percent of the profits to his investors. He promised a return that couldn't happen. He had vastly oversold the shipment—if indeed there ever was one.

He had, with great calculation, set out to take money from

those who could spare it the least, and, even worse, he kept meticulous records of all the transactions.

Eliza bolted to her feet, once again startling the cat. "Tiger," she crowed happily, lifting the kitten to her face, "that's it! He kept records! He did! And do you know what? I have them! I have them, Tiger! *I have them!*"

She pulled on her coat and carefully put the piece of paper in her pocket. She'd find a safer place for it later. Right now she had to run over and tell Silas right away.

Her feet barely skimmed the stairs as she sped down out of the boardinghouse. Vaguely she heard Mrs. Adams calling her, but she merely waved over her shoulder.

This was too important.

The lights were on in the Collier house, and she could see Silas and Edward inside. She pounded on the door, and when Silas opened it, she hugged him. "I've got it!"

From the other side of the room, Edward chuckled. "Well, if you've got it, share it!"

"Look!" She took the list out of her purse and waved it in front of Silas's face. "Look! It's Blaine's record of his transactions! I've got the proof!"

"Whoa, slow down!" Silas said. "What record? Proof of what?"

There was a knock at the door, and Hyacinth joined them. She was out of breath and quite red. "I am in no shape to go running after you, Eliza, so this had better be important. You scared me to death, running out like that."

"Oh, it's important all right," Eliza said. "Let's sit and talk."

The four of them sat at the table in the kitchen, the list in front of them. "I found this in my bag. Blaine left it in my shop, and he told me that he had an important investors meeting that evening, so I took it to his home. Unfortunately—or fortunately, I should say—I found him with another woman, and I raced home, packed my things, and left. This was in the bottom of my bag, and I didn't see it until tonight."

"Why did you have your bag out tonight?" Silas asked. "Were you—were you leaving?"

"For a while. I decided to go to St. Paul and at least tell what I knew. Silas, I think I did know, but I just didn't want to admit it, and I was coming back. Do you want me to?"

Edward shook his head. "Did you just say everything backwards? That made no sense at all."

Eliza and Silas stared at him. "She was going to give a statement in St. Paul about what she knew concerning Blaine Loring, the fellow that bilked all those young women out of their savings," Silas said. "She now thinks she knew all along what was going on. She was planning to come back to Remembrance after her statement, and yes, I want her to come back. You didn't follow all that?"

"You two are definitely meant for each other," Hyacinth said. "Nobody else could understand you. But go on. Edward and I will try to stay with you."

"Take a look at these registers," Eliza said. "If you add up the percentages, instead of coming to 100 percent, they total almost 350 percent. Do you see what he did? You can't sell 350 percent of anything because there isn't 350 percent. There can't be more than 100 percent."

"Intriguing," Edward said.

"I see," Silas said. "But what I don't understand is why he was so careless with this list at your shop. He undoubtedly considered you to be into the scheme, too."

Eliza shook her head. "I don't think so. Blaine must not have thought I could read. After all, most of the household help who'd invested couldn't read. I'm sure he showed them these lists, and the numbers, and they wouldn't have understood what they were looking at, just that they were getting back a lot of money—which of course, they were not."

"But you could read." Edward beamed happily at her.

"I can read and write and add and subtract and multiply and divide. And do percentages. But of course that wouldn't have even occurred to Blaine. He was so egotistical he'd never have even considered that someone as lowly as a seamstress could, in fact, read and understand this list."

"He sounds like quite a piece of work, this fellow does," Edward commented.

"Oh, he was that and then some. I am well rid of him."

Silas frowned. "It's not going to be easy for you. You'll probably come under a good deal of scrutiny yourself, and you may have to answer to exactly what you knew and when. Are you ready for it?"

"I have to do what I have to do." Eliza's stomach twisted as she considered what kinds of questions she might face in St. Paul. "I don't know that I'm ready for it, or even if I ever would be. But it's something I must do, and since I have this list, which is about as close to any proof as we're ever going to get, I'd say I have the responsibility to share it with the authorities."

"You could be arrested." Silas's voice cracked. "Did you think of that?"

"Of course I did. What Blaine did was horrible, and I feel guilty beyond belief for my part in it. I will do whatever I need to do to make things right."

They were brave words, but inside Eliza was quivering at the thought that her path might end in a cell. The time had come, though, for her to stop running and to put things right, not just for her but for the women he had stolen the money from.

"When do we leave?" Silas asked.

"You're going with me? You don't have to. You have things to do here in Remembrance."

"Eliza, of course I want to go with you. If you don't want me to go, you just have to say the word."

"Well, you have the Robbins house to work on, and Edward here, with his precious limb and all...."

"My what?" Edward interjected. "What on earth are you talking about? My precious limb? Could you two go back to English, please?"

"No, Silas, you should stay here. Your uncle needs you. I can go to St. Paul by myself. I used to live there, you know." As much as she would like his presence, she knew this was something she had to do on her own.

"I'll go with her," Hyacinth announced. "You two need to stay here and watch Tiger, and finish up Birdbath House so we can move in. Mrs. Adams is getting nervous. I think she's convinced herself that we're coming with her to move in with her precious Ella."

"You'll be all right, alone in the city?" Edward asked Hyacinth, grasping her hand and gazing into her eyes.

"Pudding Plum, we'll be fine."

"*Pudding Plum?*" Silas and Eliza mouthed in unison.

"We'll try to leave tomorrow," Eliza said. "Will you tell the Robbins family that I'll be back soon? If you two really want to help, you could sew the buttonholes on Luke's shirt and finish hemming Analia's dress."

"We'll watch the cat," Edward said. "I think everyone would be happiest if we left the sewing to you."

"Sounds reasonable," Eliza said, chuckling. "But I'd better get back to the boardinghouse and get ready for this trip."

"I'll walk you over there," Silas said. "Uncle Edward, you'll see Hyacinth home?"

"Of course," Edward replied. "I think I can hobble over there and back. Eliza, in case I don't see you before you leave, my prayers are with you."

"Thanks, Edward. I know I'll need them."

As they walked slowly toward the boardinghouse, Eliza took a deep breath. "There, can you smell it? It's not the January thaw this time. It's the real thing. Spring is coming. I can already smell the rain and the trees and the grass."

"I'm ready for winter to end," Silas said, taking her hand. "I don't mean just the calendar's winter either. My own winter has gone on long enough. It's time for me to find spring."

"I understand exactly," Eliza said. "I've been living in pain of one sort or the other for too long, and I've made mistakes because of it. I really need to know, Silas—can you forgive me?"

He squeezed her hand. "Being a Christian means agreeing to forgive. I've really had to work on that, because for me, anyway, it's the hardest part of following Jesus. I have to forgive. The Bible demands it of me. I fought it and fought it, but no matter how hard I struggled, I came right back to it. I have to do it. It's a gift that I get, and it's a gift I can give."

"I think it's the closest we can get to grace," she said softly. "God gives it to us freely, and we need to be able to do it, too. But it's difficult."

Silas stopped and faced her. "Eliza, I'll be honest with you. Your relationship with Blaine Loring frightened me, not just about the fact that he was a criminal, but that he was able to so completely take you over. I've never been in a romance before." He cleared his throat. "I don't think I could make you love me so much that you'd forget everything for me. I don't think I'd want to."

"God gave me a brain," she said. "I forgot to use it when I was with Blaine. I was young and I was foolish and I was so very needy. I was the perfect target for him. I don't want to be a target again."

"What do you want from the man who loves you?"

"I want him to tell me he loves me. I want him to hold me in his arms. I want him to respect me and love me and trust me and care for me."

His eyes softened in the moonlight that filtered through the trees, and as they stood together, arms around each other, Eliza knew she was home.

❧

"This has been quite an exciting time," Uncle Edward said as the train pulled away, bearing Eliza and Hyacinth on their way to St. Paul. "Eliza certainly is brave, going to the capital to give her statement. It would have been so much easier for her if she'd just let the whole thing go, but that's not our Eliza's way, is it?"

"I'm so very proud of her. I wish I were going there with her." He touched his mouth, where just minutes earlier Eliza had placed a going-away kiss. "I want her back here with me, safe and sound."

They began to walk back to their house. One of the things that Silas loved about this part of the state was that spring bounded in and pushed winter out. That was what was happening. Oh, there would still be skirmishes—there was almost always a spring blizzard or two—but for the moment, the sun was out, the air was warming, and even the birds sounded more chipper than usual.

It would have been a good day to take a walk with his Eliza.

"How do you think she's coping with all of this?" his uncle asked. His limp was almost gone, and he could now walk without expending most of his energy. Today he wasn't even using a cane.

"She was used so badly by this scoundrel, and I know she's having a hard time forgiving herself for her part in the plot. She's run through an entire laundry list of *if*s. What if she hadn't been so eager to move up in the world? What if she hadn't taken so readily to his proposal that she solicit these young women for their money?" Silas stopped, but only for a moment. There was more. "What if she hadn't found him with that other woman? Might she have stayed with him, blinded by what she thought was love, until she was entwined in his corruption?"

"If she hadn't come across them locked in an embrace, she could have stayed with him and gotten even more deeply involved, that's true," Edward considered. "Perhaps it's best that she did see that, even though it hurt her terribly. God was truly looking out for her. It does seem that sometimes He takes us through the valley only to show us the sunshine, doesn't it?"

Silas looked at his uncle. "You've become quite the poet recently."

Edward shrugged. "Blame it on love, I suppose. You'll probably take up the lute and start composing romantic ballads yourself, and I'll have to listen to you all hours of the day and night, strumming and singing your heart out."

"I don't think so," Silas said with a grin. "I'd never subject you to my singing."

"It's good to see you like this," his uncle said. "There's so much joy in being in love. I'm glad you've found it. Eliza is a wonderful woman."

Their path took them near Birdbath House, and they stopped in to see what was left to be done. Tiger, who was at the Collier house while Eliza and Hyacinth were gone, had clearly done her job well. There was no evidence of mice.

"You know what we should do?" Edward said as they

walked through the house. "Let's get this ready for them so when they come home they can move right in. We just have some cleaning and painting to do, and get this old furniture out and move the new in from the boardinghouse."

"That's all we have to do? All?" Silas surveyed the house. "I suppose I could—we *could*—in two or three days if I didn't go to the Robbins house."

"Cleaning should be the first item on the agenda." Edward ran his finger over the windowsill and held up the grimy proof. "As far as the Robbins family goes, they might like a break from the constant hammering and sawing. You'll catch up."

His uncle had an excellent point.

"All right, let's do it."

For the rest of the afternoon, the two men scrubbed and swept and polished and wiped, until the house glistened. Silas leaned against the doorjamb. It was really quite amazing what they had accomplished. "Tomorrow we'll move the old furniture out. Then we'll move the items from Mrs. Adams's place in here."

"So you think two more days?"

"That should do it. We'll be quite the pair when Eliza and Hyacinth come back into town. We'll be achingly stiff and sore."

"But it'll be worth it. I can't wait to see my petunia blossom's face when she realizes she can stay in Birdbath House."

"*Petunia blossom?* You're saying Hyacinth is a petunia blossom? Is that even botanically possible?"

Edward winked at him. "Poetic license, Silas. Poetic license."

Silas laughed.

Edward mopped the sweat from his forehead as they packed up to leave the house. "I'm clearly not as young as I once was—or as I thought I was. Whew!"

Silas studied him covertly. His uncle's knuckles were swollen with arthritis, and during this short stint of cleaning, he'd managed to cut his thumb fairly deeply, and one fingernail was going to be black after he'd dropped a picture frame on it.

It wasn't right. People you loved weren't supposed to get old and weak.

"I know, Silas." His uncle's voice was soft and understanding. "I'm not what I used to be, not on the outside, and you know, not even on the inside. Each whack I take on the outside teaches me something on the inside. That's how life goes."

"Uncle Edward—"

His uncle held up his hand and stemmed Silas's objection. "I need to say this. As you know, I'll be taking Hyacinth as my bride soon—and yes, I know you don't approve of it, but I know what's in my heart and hers, so we are getting married whether you're there or not. Over the years, I've gotten a fairly profitable carpentry business built up."

"You do excellent work, Uncle." Silas picked up a pail and began spreading out the wet rags over the edge of it.

"When I manage to stay on the ladder. Which brings me to the next point. I'm looking at some changes, not just with my marrying Hyacinth. Silas, I'm offering you the business. I'm not getting any younger, and the time has come for me to have whatever adventures are ahead, to enjoy them while I can."

"But—"

"The right answer is, 'thank you,'" Edward said. "Not 'but.' You're a good carpenter, and you've become like my own son. I'm proud to pass the business on to you. . .if you want it. I'm hoping you'll say yes."

Silas put the pail down and looked at his uncle. In his face he saw the man who took in the untaught teenager, spent hour after hour, day after day, teaching him the ways of the wood, and all the time putting his own life on hold.

Was he the reason his uncle had never married before?

"Thank you," he said, and reached out, giving his uncle a long-overdue hug.

∂

Silas looked up at the stars. His uncle had already gone to bed, and Silas was a bit concerned about the way Edward had winced on the stairs. He'd done too much too soon.

The stairs hadn't been easy for him, either, and he was thirty-something years younger than his uncle. They'd worked hard and they'd worked long today, and now they were going to pay for it.

Silas groaned as he thought of what he'd feel like in the morning. And he'd scheduled them to move the furniture out!

Would he be able to sleep tonight? His body needed rest, but his mind wouldn't stop turning over the conversation at Birdbath House.

He had the carpentry business. His future was secured.

He picked up *Professor Barkley's Patented Five Year Plan for Success*. What did the professor have in store for him today? He opened and began to read.

What have you left undone? Is there something that you've been ignoring because you simply don't want to see it? Maybe it's a pile of papers on your desk. Or a stain on the rug near the door? That missing button on your coat?

Or is it more than that? Is there an apology you've been avoiding? Do you have some anger that you need to diffuse? Some ill will that's taken root in your soul so deeply that it's going to be painful to pull it out?

Today, deal with what you have put aside for later. It is later.

Memory verse—Proverbs 3:27: Withhold not good from them to whom it is due, when it is in the power of thine hand to do it.

Well, that was an odd little entry, and it certainly didn't fit into the day, not at all.

He read through the memory verse until he had it learned, and then, after his prayers, he slipped into his bed. As he fell into sleep, Professor Barkley's words taunted him. What had he left undone?

It was, he decided, another one of the professor's puzzles. Remembering what one had forgotten was about as easy as expecting the unexpected.

He'd never figure it out.

eleven

Eliza and Hyacinth stood in front of the police station. A light spring snow was falling that melted as soon as it touched the ground. "I don't know if this is the right place or not," Eliza said, "but there's only one way to find out. Are you ready?"

"Let's say a prayer first," Hyacinth suggested, and the two women stepped to the side and, holding hands, dropped their heads. "Dearest God, we ask that You guide Eliza's words and actions now, in His name, Amen."

Eliza laughed. "Short but effective."

"We can hope. Shall we go in?"

After being sent from one desk to another and speaking to a series of law enforcement officials, they finally ended up speaking to the chief of police, a kind-looking man with a thick white moustache. He listened closely to Eliza and asked questions, but mainly he let her tell her story.

She handed him the list of the names of the "investors" and their promised returns and watched as he studied it. At last he nodded. "This appears to be exactly the document we need. With the name of the unfortunates he took advantage of, we'll be able to gather even more witnesses."

"I wish something could be done for these young women who were take advantage of," Eliza said. "I know they'll all be grateful to see him behind bars, but that's a small cold comfort when you've lost your money."

The chief smiled. "Come to find out, Loring has quite

the eye for art. His collection is worth quite a bit of money. I wouldn't be at all surprised to hear the court order it to be sold, and the profits distributed among the women. After all, it was their money that purchased the items." He smiled at her. "I believe that would be equitable."

She nodded. "I see. I'm glad to hear that. It makes this all a bit easier to accept, knowing that my friends will see at least some recouping of their losses."

He stood up. "Thank you very much for coming forward, Miss Davis. You are extraordinarily brave."

He shook her hand, and then Hyacinth's, and guided them to the exit. Eliza paused for a moment, long enough to let her knees stop shaking, and she heard the chief call to the captain, "Come to my office. We've got him now! Loring is ours!"

She looked at Hyacinth and smiled. "He believed me."

"You must feel relieved that it's all over," Hyacinth said to her.

"It's not quite over. I have some apologies to make."

Eliza led Hyacinth to her old neighborhood. Most of the women she knew were still there, and to her delight, they listened readily to her story and forgave her. "We knew your heart," one of them, a soft-spoken nanny, said to her. "You would never have hurt us on purpose."

"I have some things of yours," another said, her apron and cap indicating kitchen service. "We heard that the Loring fellow was going to go through your shop and your home— what he was looking for, I don't know, but it wasn't right. So some of us went to the shop and some to your quarters, and we got out what we could."

A third woman, her hands crusted from the harsh soaps she used to clean, added, "His men aren't so tough. They took one look at us, and they tucked tail and ran, like a bunch of mangy curs."

The group laughed, and the cook led them to the store-room where in a box were the rest of Eliza's clothes, all neatly folded, and the rest of her sewing materials. "And behind here, I've got your machine." The cook opened a cupboard, and in it sat Eliza's sewing machine, dismantled to fit, but all there.

"You are all absolutely the best!" Eliza hugged each one of them. "I'll take these with me now, but you all must promise me that if you ever can get to Remembrance, you'll come and see me. Promise?"

There was nothing quite like good friends, she thought as she surveyed the group of women she'd known before, and Hyacinth, who came all this way for her. Friends made all the difference.

And now it was time for her to be a friend, as she took Hyacinth to her favorite store to buy some lovely yellow silk for her wedding dress, white lace bands for the sleeves and neck, and pearl buttons to march down the back in a tidy row. She couldn't wait to start on it.

As she sat on the train coming back, Hyacinth snoring softly at her side, she took stock of herself. She was finally happy, and her spiritual housecleaning was well underway. She'd cleared out the dirt and the webs and flung open the doors to let the sunshine in.

Her life was taking shape at last.

❧

"Do you see them yet?"

"No, Silas, not yet." Uncle Edward walked with only a faint limp, but today he was using the cane again. All the bustle to get the house ready for the women had taken its toll. "But soon. I think I heard it a minute ago."

The station was empty. There wasn't much call for the train to stop in Remembrance. Usually materials for the store were the only reason that the train even slowed down.

"Silas, since your own dear father long ago left his earth for his heavenly reward, I feel I should be the one to talk to you about love."

Silas laughed. "You? But you're Pudding Plum, as I recall. It seems to me that anyone who lets himself be called Pudding Plum is in no position to advise anyone else."

"You'll see, Silas. One day Eliza will call you something equally as ridiculous, like Lovey Lamb, and you'll absolutely melt. That's the way it is with love."

"Lovey Lamb?" Silas shuddered. "Oh, spare me!"

"I'm serious. If anyone else were to call you that, you'd probably straighten him right out. But because it's the woman you love, you'll smile and get fluttery and although you'll be as embarrassed as anything, you'll treasure it."

"I can't see Eliza doing that."

"Just wait. You never know. You'll be at church or with a customer, and she'll come in and she'll call you Lovey Lamb, and you'll want to sink through the floor—but you'll be as proud as anything that it's *you* she called Lovey Lamb."

"Lovey Lamb? Honestly, Uncle Edward, Eliza?"

His uncle chuckled. "Maybe not. But, Silas, you need to be able to have fun with the woman you love. Enjoy her company. Share laughter. Have secret jokes that belong to just the two of you. Remember that in marriage, two have become one."

"Uncle Edward, aren't you jumping ahead just a little bit? Or maybe a whole lot? You've got Eliza and me getting married. Don't you think we ought to court a little while?" Silas grinned.

The sound of the train came closer.

"Isn't that what you two have been doing?" his uncle responded. "You two learn to talk and laugh and not get so caught up in your own pride, and you'll be ready to marry."

"I think I'll wait a little bit, if you don't mind."

"You know what you need to do?" Uncle Edward asked.

The *chicketta-ticketta* of the train grew even louder, and his heart beat faster at the thought that she'd soon be in Remembrance.

"What do I need to do, Uncle?" Silas asked.

The train was too loud for him to hear his answer clearly, but it sounded for all the world like, "Kiss her."

He was never one to ignore good advice. The minute she stepped onto the platform, he swung her into his arms and kissed her squarely on the lips.

For a kiss that was tinged with locomotive smoke and grit, it wasn't bad at all. But just in case it could get better, he kissed her again. And again. And again.

❧

The children crowded around Eliza. "This is a sewing machine," she said, letting them each look at it. "When I move the crank on this wheel like this, see how the needle goes up and down?"

The children were transfixed by the machine that Eliza set up in the Robbins home for the day. Silas carried it over in its wooden carrying case. They'd never seen anything like it. Analia stood at Eliza's shoulder, Tiger cradled in her arms.

"But just having the needle go up and down isn't enough with a machine, even though it is with hand sewing. For a machine to make a stitch, two threads are required, and that's what this little shuttle under here is for. It loops with the thread from up above to make the stitch. Now watch. I'm going to sew this seam."

She put the gown she was making for Mrs. Robbins in place and within a minute had the seam sewn. "Compare that to how long it takes me to hand stitch a seam, and you can understand why we take very good care of our sewing machines."

"Wouldn't it be nice," Silas said from the other side of the room where he was still putting up cupboards, "if someday someone would invent a machine that could put nails in place as easily as that puts stitches in? Then I could stand here, and instead of hammering in each nail, I could simply *pop-pop-pop-pop* them into place."

"Not likely to ever happen," Luke commented. "That's just dangerous."

Eliza looked up and smiled surreptitiously at Silas. Luke was very sweet, but very ten years old. He was at the age in which he knew it all, or at least most of it.

"Well, if they do invent a nail machine, I'll be the first in line to buy one. This hammering all day long is really hard on my arms." He rubbed his right shoulder.

"If you need help," little Mark offered, "I'm very good at pounding nails."

"Thank you, Mark. I'll keep that in mind."

The staccato hammering and the whirr of the sewing machine blended to make a solid background noise that, at least momentarily, drowned out the constant chatter of the children.

Having the machine back made so much difference, she thought, as the boys' shirts almost finished themselves. This had to be one of the best inventions created.

Once her world had tilted upside down. Now it was being righted, and it was wonderful. She took stock of all that had happened for the good.

She had fallen in love. That was the best, of course. When she first met him, he'd been so solemn, his eyes studiously serious behind his wire-rimmed glasses. Now, he'd come out of his own shadow, and she enjoyed being with him so much that loving him came easily.

She had a friend. How could she have gone on without Hyacinth at her side, advising and supporting her all the way? She had a sewing machine. She had a cat. She even had a house now, at least for a while. Hyacinth had added some charming touches to Birdbath House, so it truly felt like home.

Plus spring was definitely in the air. The snow and ice had begun to melt at an amazing rate, so that walking under any eaves or awnings meant sure splatters of water on one's head. Even the birds seemed happier.

Mary Robbins had actually gotten out of bed and come into the front room twice. The doctor told her that if she continued to regain her strength, she'd be back to health by summer's end.

Tomorrow Eliza would start on Hyacinth's wedding dress. The date was set for the first Sunday in June, right after the church services. All of Remembrance was invited, and even Mrs. Adams said she'd try to come back for it. She'd left four days ago, and Hyacinth and Eliza were reveling in having their dinner at 12:01 or even 12:02.

All in all, everything was perfect. Couldn't be better. Nothing to change.

Hyacinth came out of Mary's room after visiting with her, and Eliza stopped the machine to talk to her. Hyacinth smiled widely. "I think Mary's going to come to the wedding! She said she wants to but she doesn't have anything to wear. Eliza, do you think you could—"

Silas's nail-pounding stopped, and he laid the hammer on

the table with a bit more emphasis than necessary.

"Eliza, I'm going to talk to Edward. I'll see you back at Birdbath House," Hyacinth said in a low voice, her eyes guardedly watching Silas.

Eliza nodded.

A pin that had been stuck into the fabric imperfectly worked its way loose and jabbed her finger. A bright spot of blood appeared, and she wiped it away before it could spot the fabric.

She needed to pay closer attention. That was simply a pin, but if she were careless around the machine, she could do much worse damage to her hands. She hadn't had it happen, but she'd seen it often enough with the other seamstresses, their hands riddled with scars from just such accidents.

It was a good thing this was Saturday. Tomorrow she'd be able to sit in church, soaking up the Word, and generally getting good with the Lord again. Sundays were her day of rejuvenation, and she certainly needed it.

Silas had stopped hammering and was now measuring the hinge placement. He measured, marked, re-measured, re-marked, over and over until at last he gave up with a sigh.

"How close are you to being done?" he asked.

"I can finish these shirts at home. There's just a bit left on each. Want to help me take the machine to the wagon?"

He strode over and began to insert the machine into its wooden table case with quick short movements. She clamped her lips together and folded the remaining items to take with her, and stopped into Mary's room to retrieve the cat.

The woman was sitting up in bed, looking better than she had all winter. Her hair was washed and braided, the work of Hyacinth who made sure that Mary looked as good—or better—than she felt.

"I hear you would like a new dress," Eliza said as she unhooked Tiger's claws from the blanket. "Any particular color or style?"

"You've already done too much," Mary protested, but Eliza waved her objection away.

"Making a dress is very easy for me. It won't take long at all. Just tell me what color you'd like. You can't have yellow since Hyacinth will be wearing a stunning yellow wedding dress. Red might be a bit too vivid, and black's harsh. How about a sky blue or a summer green or even a lilac or lavender?"

"Oh, I do like lavender. Let me get Jack in here to pay you—"

"No, no payment. I brought back my sewing machine and trunk that I left in St. Paul, and there's a nice length of fabric that I think will be perfect on you. The background is lavender, and there are tiny sprigs of flowers in creamy ivory. So, the next question is the style. What would you like?"

"Can you select something for me? You have so much more experience than I have."

"It would be an honor."

Eliza carried the cat to the wagon, and when they got in, Silas burst out with, "I'm sorry. I just can't deal with them getting married. I think it's wrong."

She faced him square on. "Get over it. They're in love. What's wrong with that?"

"We've already gone over this. They met through letters. She came out here without having ever even seen him. Don't you think that's odd?" He frowned.

"It's not the way I would do it, but on the other hand, I'm not Hyacinth. I'm not an older widow whose options for finding love again are limited."

"But to do it that way?"

"What do you care how they met? It's working out. Take a look at them, Silas. Pudding Plum is madly in love with his morning flower. Sappy, I agree, but look at how contented they are. Who cares how they got there? Why are you so upset?"

"I'm afraid," he said at last, "that I'm to blame for this. If Uncle Edward hadn't taken me in when I was a young man, he would have had time to meet someone else, and he'd have gotten married and—"

"He *might* have met someone. He *might* have gotten married." She shook her head. "Besides, everything is turning out just fine. He's retiring—and getting off ladders—and he's passing the carpentry business on to you. He's in love. What's wrong with that? It sounds good to me."

His lips tightened again into that expression that she'd seen way too much of, and she knew what it meant. He had an opinion, and he was going to hold onto it until it was forced out of his grasp.

"It's not the way we do things here," he said.

"It's not the way anybody does things—except for these two. Just be glad for them. They found each other, and I can't imagine two people who seem to be better suited for each other than them."

It was true. They were completely and totally ideal as a couple.

"I don't want him to be hurt," he said after a long silence.

"I don't think he will be," she replied honestly. "I suspect that your treatment of the woman he loves hurts him more than anything right now."

He stared straight ahead, his jaw clenched.

"Just take me home, Silas," she finished gently. "Help me

unload the sewing machine and get it set up in Birdbath House, and you can go think about this. It's really vital for you to work this out inside your soul." She took a deep breath. "Until you do, I don't think you and I can go further. It's too big and too important for you to walk around with this weight in your heart."

He said no more than the necessary words as he set up her machine in the house for her and left again. She stood at the window and watched him go. He'd never looked so lonely.

And she'd never felt so lonely.

❧

He'd gotten far behind with his readings from *Professor Barkley's Patented Five Year Plan for Success*, and he took the book out to catch up. Perhaps the professor had some advice for him.

But the daily lessons were more of the same. *Be careful what you say.* He tried to be cautious with his speech. If he felt he was losing control, he simply opted for silence. *Be kind to those less fortunate.* Look at how much time he spent at the Robbins house. *Pray for peace.* Well, that was a given.

Could it be that Professor Barkley was getting—more predictable?

Maybe it was time for another list. He did enjoy lists. He glanced at his Bible, where his list of questions for Eliza was safely tucked away. Maybe his lists weren't always as helpful as he hoped, but they helped him organize his thoughts.

He made two columns on a piece of paper. One column he titled, *YEAS*. The other, *NAYS*.

He worked on his columns until he could come up with nothing else, and he leaned back and studied the results.

Under the *YEAS* were two entries: *They seem to love each other*, and *They seem to make each other happy*.

Under the *NAYS* were also two entries: *They don't really know each other*, and *They act crazy*.

So it hadn't been a particularly fruitful exercise. He expected more from it. His head wasn't any clearer than before. He wadded up the list and threw it toward the wastebasket, missing it entirely—something, he noted wryly, he had done a lot of lately.

He lowered his head and stared at the wall. Since when did someone have to like everybody? Well, there was of course the biblical injunction that *Thou shalt love thy neighbour as thyself*, but did that really apply here? He searched for the phrase in his Bible, and soon sat back, shaking his head.

It was from Matthew 22, the same chapter that Reverend Tupper had used as his text in church a while back. The verse about loving his neighbor came after the wedding feast story, and according to Jesus, it was a foundational premise. He read it again: *Then one of them, which was a lawyer, asked him a question, tempting him, and saying, Master, which is the great commandment in the law? Jesus said unto him, Thou shalt love the Lord thy God with all thy heart, and with all thy soul, and with all thy mind. This is the first and great commandment. And the second is like unto it, Thou shalt love thy neighbour as thyself. On these two commandments hang all the law and the prophets.*

That last line laid a heavy responsibility on him. Clearly the charge to love others wasn't minor at all. Jesus compared it to loving God Himself.

His head started to hurt. Being a Christian was getting increasingly complicated. If Hyacinth and Eliza hadn't shown up in Remembrance, he might have been able to sail on through the rest of his life without these challenges. But now, having heard the Word on the subject, he had no choice but adapt his life.

That meant loving Hyacinth. Was it possible? If God insisted, could he?

He got up from the table and laid his weary body on his bed. Why did life have to be so complicated? His head pounded even harder. His eyes closed against the pain, and at last he slipped into a restless sleep.

His fitful dreams were interrupted by his uncle hollering up the stairs at him. "Are you going to church or have you turned into a heathen?" Silas's eyes flew open to glaring daylight and he groaned. If his uncle was already up and anxious about church, he must have overslept. He swung his legs over the side of the bed and stood up, automatically checking the weather outside his window as he did so.

It was a beautiful Sunday morning, and he winced at the sun's beams. The way he felt, at the very least the weather could have cooperated and produced some thundering clouds to gray up the sky.

But Sunday was Sunday, and he didn't miss church. He cleaned himself quickly and pulled on good clothes and headed downstairs. His uncle was already at the stove, and he handed Silas a plate of ham and eggs.

"Wolf this down and let's get going. I don't want to be late."

Silas ate as quickly as he could, and soon the two men were headed into the church.

Edward of course greeted Hyacinth enthusiastically. Today, she was his Sparkling Sunday Sunbeam. Silas tried very hard not to react. He was going to make every attempt to be kind to her.

Eliza was polite but guarded as he slid into the pew next to her. "Let's talk after church," he whispered to her as they stood for the first hymn, and she nodded. He had no idea what he was going to say to her. Perhaps something would come to him during church.

He sat back in the pew, mulling over the upcoming discussion with Eliza, when the sermon began. Reverend Tupper was in fine form, delivering a rousing sermon based upon Proverbs 22:24. Silas found himself listening intently, and he hung on every word.

"Make no friendship with an angry man." As the minister proceeded to explain the wisdom of the proverb, why one should choose one's companions carefully, Silas considered another angle of it.

What if he was the angry man?

Certainly he'd been polite enough—outwardly—with his uncle's romance, but lately he'd become aware that it had blown into something more virulent. He'd become angry about it.

Was Eliza thinking the same thing? Was she concerned about the man next to her, the man she'd professed to love? He was the angry man—and the Bible warned others about him.

He felt as if he'd been brought up sharp in front of God and had been found wanting.

But what was he to do? He had to make some change, somehow. He needed to let the anger go. The fact was, though, that it was one thing to be aware of it, but something else entirely to be able to do it.

He squeezed his eyes shut and prayed, asking God to take away his anger, to clean his heart of these negative emotions. If he was going to be able to love, he had to have an anger-free heart.

He prayed longer. More intently. He didn't want to carry this burden of hate any longer. He wanted it gone.

The fact was, he realized as he continued to petition God, he nurtured his dislike of Hyacinth. He looked for fault at every turn. His scorn became his pet, his companion, and he elevated it into a consuming passion that froze his heart to her. In other words, it had nothing to do with Hyacinth, and everything to do with him. His heart was in desperate need of a good housecleaning. He opened the darkness of his soul to the light of God's goodness and aired out every corner.

Bit by bit, he felt the ice leave the haven he'd given it in his heart, and his soul was filled again with joy.

After church, he and Eliza walked the short distance to Birdbath House. The snow was almost gone, and they had to pick their way through the rutted mud.

"I was the angry man," he said, "but I've made a commitment not to be. You were right. I needed to let go of my dislike of Hyacinth. For one thing, I was so concerned about my own future here in Remembrance that I let my worries overtake my senses. Plus I was being too protective of my uncle, and he is, after all, quite the grown man and able to make his own decisions. I still think it's a crazy way to find someone to love, but if it worked, then praise God."

"I'm glad," she said, taking his arm as they reached a particularly muddy area. "I do think you'll find Hyacinth to be quite a wonderful woman, very worthy of your uncle's love."

"You mean Pudding Plum and—what did he call her this morning?—Sparkling Sunday Sunbeam are meant for each other?"

"I do."

"Are we?" He held his breath, waiting for her answer.

She stopped and put her hands on each side of his face. "We

are." She stood on tiptoe and kissed him. "And I promise I'll never call you names like that. Not Honey Bee. Not Darling Dumpling. And never," she finished, grinning impishly, "Lovey Lamb."

twelve

"I told her about it," Uncle Edward confessed when Silas asked him how she knew about "Lovey Lamb" from the earlier conversation the men had. "I thought she might find a time to use it," he added, grinning, "and I gather she did."

Silas laughed. "She did. But she did promise never to call me Lovey Lamb, so in the long run it was worth it."

His uncle shook his head. "Never underestimate the power of a bit of silly affection."

"Why, Uncle, you sound like quite the romantic expert," Silas quipped, raising his eyebrows in mock surprise. "For someone who avoided marriage for your entire life thus far, you sure do seem to know the secrets of a happy relationship. Is there something you haven't told me?"

Uncle Edward chuckled. "Probably. Oh, speaking of things I haven't told you, Hyacinth and I've decided not to move to Duluth, but to stay here."

"I'm delighted, of course, to hear that you'll stay here, but I thought your dream was to move to Duluth," Silas said. He marveled at his calm. Whatever the change in plans boded for his life, God was in charge.

His uncle shrugged. "Remembrance is home. Besides, moving is work for people my age, and I don't think I'm up for it. Plus I can do my work here as well as I could in Duluth."

"I thought you were retiring." Silas frowned. His uncle's hands weren't as steady as they used to be, and in woodworking, steady hands were all-important. It simply wasn't safe for

Uncle Edward to continue to work with the sharp tools, and making his products to his demanding standards would be difficult.

"Oh, I'm giving the carpentry business over to you, no doubt about that. I mean my writing. I can do that anywhere."

"Writing?" Silas gaped at his uncle. "You want to be a writer? I had no idea!"

"Oh, I already am. About ten years ago I wrote some silly thing called *Professor Barkley's Patented Five Year Plan for Success*." Uncle Edward frowned a bit. "This is one of those things I didn't tell you, apparently. Well, it wasn't some grand production. I put all the sensible advice I could come up with into a book, and it sold, oh, maybe fifteen or twenty copies." He grinned. "I think I might rewrite it, update it for the new era, you know."

"You wrote it? You're Professor Barkley?"

His uncle laughed. "You can't tell me you've heard of it."

"Heard of it? I've been reading it every night for the past nine months. I found a copy in my room when I moved the nightstand—it was under the drawer in it, wedged in there pretty soundly."

"Oh, that's where I put the book. I looked all over the place for it. I think it's time for a revision, don't you?"

Silas laughed. "You might consider taking out all the warnings about romantic entanglements."

"You're right. I need to encourage love. After all, doesn't the Good Book say in the Song of Solomon, 'This is my beloved, and this is my friend'? How can anyone have a plan for success without including love?"

How, indeed? How, indeed!

❧

Snowflakes sparkled in the moonlight as Eliza and Silas

lingered outside Birdbath House. Hyacinth and Edward were inside, cleaning up after the dinner the four of them had shared.

"What do you think Mrs. Adams would say about that?" he asked, indicating the silhouettes of the older couple in the window as they shared a quick kiss over a pan of dishes.

"I think she'd say they should get married, and quickly."

Eliza felt as full as a cat. If she were able, she would have purred. The dinner of roast chicken and biscuits had been delicious, and sleep threatened to overtake her. She fought back a yawn. Had she ever been this happy?

"That's a splendid idea." He put his hands on her shoulders and turned her to face him. "Eliza, shall we make it a double wedding?"

Her sleepiness vanished. "A double—do you mean—are you saying what I think you're saying?"

"I should do this properly." He dropped to one knee and took her gloved hand in his. "We haven't known each other long, but the heart has its own schedule. I've loved you from the first time I saw you. You were scented with blueberries and soap, and you literally fell into my arms. I want you by my side—and in my arms—for the rest of my life."

She couldn't answer. Her heart caromed in her chest, coming to land squarely in her throat.

"I thought that *Professor Barkley's Patented Five Year Plan for Success* was going to revolutionize my life, but it didn't take into account one thing—and that was love."

"Professor Barkley's what?"

He waved her question away. "I'll explain later. So, Eliza, will you?"

"Will I—?" The snowflakes spun in a dizzying whirl of fairy dust.

"Oh, I still haven't asked you, have I?" Silas's cider-colored eyes shone behind his glasses. "Eliza, will you marry me?"

Everything changed. The moon glowed brighter; the stars glittered with a brilliant light. The leafless tree branches waved their approval in the evening breeze, and the flutter of wings and the hoot of an owl became a melody that floated on the night air.

"Yes," she responded, not sure if she were whispering or shouting. "Yes, yes, yes!"

He rose to his feet and wrapped her in his arms. "I love you, Eliza. Here, with God as my witness, I promise to love you always. Our love together, our life together, is just beginning."

A double wedding. What could be more perfect?

&

"You're sure, aren't you?" Uncle Edward asked his nephew.

"I am." Silas leaned against the doorjamb. It had been a magical evening, and he was reluctant to let it end. After he and Eliza had told Hyacinth and his uncle the news of their engagement and suggested the double wedding, the plans began to spin out from all four of them with great speed.

An August wedding, they decided, would be ideal. They wouldn't be rushing into their marriages, and they would have time to finalize living arrangements and the final transfer of the business.

They'd be married, of course, in the church in Remembrance, with Hyacinth and Edward taking a long honeymoon trip to Duluth. The lakeshore would be a nice setting for a post-wedding vacation.

"How could two bachelors-for-life like ourselves have ended up with such extraordinary women?" Uncle Edward mused. "In this great huge world, and in this tiny little town, how did such a marvelous thing happen?"

Sometimes, Silas thought, a Patented Five Year Plan was a good thing, but even Professor Barkley couldn't create a better system than their heavenly Father already had.

Silas looked upward and smiled. "God knows. God knows."

❧

Bees buzzed lazily in the hot August sun, but inside the church, Eliza was in a tizzy. Just minutes ago she'd had her bouquet of flowers, tied with blue string to match the new Bible Silas had given her as a wedding gift. But now the flowers were gone, and the ceremony was about to start.

"Look again," she told Hyacinth. "Maybe I left them in the wagon?"

"They're not there. I already looked. Are you sure you brought them with you?"

"I know I did. I had them with me when I got in, because a bee was overly interested in the daisies so I battled it the entire way over." Eliza put her hands on her hips and surveyed the back of the church. "They can't be that hard to find. This church isn't very big."

A sound under the pew made the two women step backward. They'd had the doors open for almost an hour now, and obviously some animal had joined them.

"Oh, please don't let it be a skunk," Eliza said. "Can you imagine what would happen if—"

At that moment Tiger stepped out, pulling the now be-draggled bouquet in her teeth. Eliza reached down and rescued the flowers. "How did you get over here?" she asked as she picked the cat up.

A small face poked around the corner. "I thought Tiger should be here," little Mark Robbins said. "I'll bet Tiger hasn't been to any weddings."

"There's a reason for that," Eliza said. "Did you go over to

Birdbath House to get her?"

He shook his head solemnly. "I think she has a secret door or something because she keeps getting out and coming to our house. I tell her she's not supposed to do that, but she doesn't listen. I think maybe it's because she likes my mother. Or me."

She had a sudden inspiration. "Mark, do you know what a wedding gift is?"

"I sure do." His face fell. "I don't have one for you."

"But I have for *you*! Mark, do you think you could take care of Tiger for always?"

"You're giving her to me? Really?"

"She's for all of you. She's now Tiger Robbins. Isn't that a great name?"

The little boy hugged the cat. "Thank you, Miss Davis! Oh, you still are Miss Davis, aren't you? You're not Mrs. Collier yet?"

"I'm still Miss Davis. But you'd better run home. You've got to come back here with your family for my wedding! And make sure that Tiger doesn't get out again."

He left, grinning from ear to ear and talking constantly to the cat. "And you can sleep in my bed on Tuesdays, and Brian's on Wednesdays. . . ."

Hyacinth smiled. "You're giving up Tiger?"

"She's over there all the time anyway, so I might as well. Plus we got another wedding present last night. Carl brought us Slick Tom. Apparently the cat liked living in town and has moped around since we took him back to the farm, so he's ours now. Just let any mouse try to drop by for a visit!"

Suddenly the church began to fill with sound as the wedding guests arrived. Hyacinth and Eliza hustled into the tiny room at the back.

"Not too much longer," Hyacinth said. "Honey, are you through trying to shred that bouquet?"

"First the cat, and now me." Eliza's fingers trembled as she tried to save the bouquet. "Hyacinth, were you this nervous before your wedding to Mr. Mason?"

"My knees were knocking together so hard I was sure people could hear them," the older woman said. "I was so fidgety that I didn't even remember the ceremony. Suddenly someone was pronouncing us man and wife, and that was it. I guess I promised the usual things, although I could have vowed to plow the fields all the days of my life, since I didn't hear any of it."

Eliza moaned. "Oh, I am so nervous!"

"There, there," Hyacinth said soothingly. "Soon it'll all be done with, and you'll go on as Mrs. Silas Collier, and I'll be Mrs. Edward Collier."

"It has a lovely sound, doesn't it?" Eliza laid the repaired bouquet on the Bible. "Any last-minute tips for me?"

"Love is fun. There's less of the drama that came during courtship, and you'll find yourself being settled in. It's good. Enjoy yourself, Eliza. Silas is a good man."

Sounds at the door announced that the wedding would shortly be underway. "Hyacinth, I have never been so scared in my life." Eliza picked up the bouquet and knotted and re-knotted the ribbons.

Reverend Tupper popped his head in. "I think it's time we proceeded with the ceremony."

One last hug, and the two brides stood together, their hands clasped together.

I'm getting married, Eliza said to herself. *I'm getting married! Thank You, dearest God, for bringing Silas and me together.* Hyacinth squeezed her hand, and Eliza added, *And for giving Hyacinth and Edward to each other.*

The Robbins family, including Mary in her lavender dress with the ivory flowers, clattered in, despite the father's admonitions for silence. "Sorry," he said in a low voice. "That cat—"

"No need to explain," Hyacinth said with a laugh.

Eliza noted the suspicious bulge in Mark's shirt. Tiger apparently had made it to the ceremony after all. She chose to ignore the furry guest. "We haven't started yet. Analia, here's your basket. Remember, you lead us off."

Analia went first, dropping wildflower petals along the aisle of church. Behind her floated Hyacinth, resplendent in her yellow silk dress with the lace edging and pearl buttons.

Eliza followed her. Now she knew why brides carried bouquets. It gave them something to hold onto so their hands could stop shaking.

Silas stepped from the side and met her in front of the altar. Her husband.

The wedding ceremony was a blur. Suddenly Reverend Tupper declared them to be husband and wife, Silas was kissing her, and she was married.

Just like that.

&

"I think Hyacinth got her good love story and her happy ending," Eliza said after the wedding, when they waved good-bye to Edward and Hyacinth, who were leaving for their honeymoon in Duluth. "What more could anyone want?"

"We do have it good," he said, putting his arm around her waist. "Think how well it all turned out. Edward and Hyacinth aren't moving to Duluth after all. They'll stay here. I like that."

As the wagon carrying Hyacinth and Edward disappeared

in the distance, they walked back to the house.

"You know," Silas said, "they're so happy together, even if they do get silly sometimes. I guess that's a blessing of its own, isn't it?"

"Speaking of silly, what did you do with *Professor Barkley's Patented Five Year Plan for Success*?"

He leaned over and kissed her. "I've got my own plan for success. It's called love."

A Letter To Our Readers

Dear Reader:

In order that we might better contribute to your reading enjoyment, we would appreciate your taking a few minutes to respond to the following questions. We welcome your comments and read each form and letter we receive. When completed, please return to the following:

Fiction Editor
Heartsong Presents
PO Box 719
Uhrichsville, Ohio 44683

1. Did you enjoy reading *Remembrance* by Janet Spaeth?
   ❑ Very much! I would like to see more books by this author!
   ❑ Moderately. I would have enjoyed it more if

   _____

   _____

   _____

2. Are you a member of **Heartsong Presents**? ❑ Yes ❑ No
   If no, where did you purchase this book? _____

   _____

3. How would you rate, on a scale from 1 (poor) to 5 (superior), the cover design? _____

4. On a scale from 1 (poor) to 10 (superior), please rate the following elements.

   ____ Heroine   ____ Plot
   ____ Hero   ____ Inspirational theme
   ____ Setting   ____ Secondary characters

5. These characters were special because? _____

_____

_____

6. How has this book inspired your life? _____

_____

_____

7. What settings would you like to see covered in future
   Heartsong Presents books? _____

_____

_____

8. What are some inspirational themes you would like to see
   treated in future books? _____

_____

_____

9. Would you be interested in reading other **Heartsong
   Presents** titles? ☐ Yes ☐ No

10. Please check your age range:
    ☐ Under 18   ☐ 18-24
    ☐ 25-34   ☐ 35-45
    ☐ 46-55   ☐ Over 55

Name _____

Occupation _____

Address _____

City, State, Zip_____

BLUE RIDGE BRIDES

3 stories in 1

Love is a challenging adventure in North Carolina. Three woman stumble onto romance amid the wilds, towns, and hollers of North Carolina. Will these women find firm footing on the road to love and marriage?

Historical, paperback, 352 pages, 5³⁄₁₆" x 8"

_____

Heart♥ng